Stories from
THE ROAD
NOT TAKEN

To Jennifer
With Best Wishes.
— Hy Hurt.

HENRY HURT

This book is a work of fiction. Names, characters, places and incidents
are the product of the author's imagination or are used fictitiously.
Any resemblance to actual events, locales or persons, living or dead, is
coincidental. The views expressed here are solely those of the author.

Copyright © 2016 Henry Hurt

ISBN: 978-0-6926-7098-9

Published in the United States of America by Shadetree Rare Books, LLC
Cover image by Thinkstock

Author contact: hhurt@shadetreerarebooks.com

First Edition: August, 2016

Books by Henry Hurt

Stories from the Road Not Taken
Shadrin: The Spy Who Never Came Back
Reasonable Doubt: An Investigation into the Assassination of John F. Kennedy

Some Major Features for Reader's Digest Magazine

"A Monster Called Mitch" (Guatemala/Honduras/Nicaragua)
"Little Boy Blue of Chester, Nebraska"
"Shame on American Soil" (Saipan, Northern Marianas/labor horrors)
"Portrait of a Patriot" (Munich/Paris/Washington/Robert Stethem)
"Hotel Fire: Cage of Horror" (Puerto Rico)
"Is This American a Soviet Spy?" (Washington/Yuri Nosenko)
"Cabin on the Hill" (Southside Virginia)
"Deliver Us from Evil" (Haiti/Indiana)
"8.0 Earthquake!" (Gujarat, India)
"And A Little Child Shall Lead Them" (Philippines)
"Horror in the Heartland" (Oklahoma City bombing)
"Search for a Terrorist Gang" (New Jersey/Thomas Manning)
"Crisis at the CIA" (William Kampiles case)
"Night of Terror, Night of Mercy" (U. S. tornados)
"An Angel on High" (Angel Wallenda)
"The Capture of Susan Lisa Rosenberg" (domestic terrorist)
"Miracle in the Blizzard" (Denver air crash)
"The Boy Who Never Came Home" (Minnesota/Jacob Wetterling)
"Red River Rising" (Grand Forks, North Dakota/Winnipeg)
"Slaughter at Albemarle Farm" (Virginia)
"Who Will Love the Children?" or "Legacy of Love" (Iowa)
"She Gave Her Father Life" (Michigan teen-aged daughter-to-father heart transplant)
"Home of the Brave" (Jerome Peirce/Civil War)
"Ring of Truth" (World War II/Soviet Union)
"Free to Kill" (North Carolina rape-murder of Amy Jackson)
"Nightmare on Nimitz Freeway" (San Francisco earthquake)
"Found: The Lost Children of Saigon"
"Murder of a Gentle Lady" (Washington)
"A Boy, a Snake and an Angel" (Florida)

Contents

Prologue

Our lives are filled with roads taken and roads not taken. You can only see the major forks when you've been around long enough to look back and put them in perspective. Nearly every major juncture--marriage, jobs, houses, children, pets, and on and on--requires us to choose one path over another. These choices set directions that guide us through our lives.

Back in the early Sixties, when I set off from Chatham, Virginia, the only sure trick in my pocket was an ability to write in an orderly way--thanks first to Charles Pace, a teacher who fiercely demanded near-perfection in diagramming sentences. Later, in high school, a teacher named Granville Smith insisted that I could write—an endearing encouragement for a lackluster pupil.

In addition to a house full of books, our family in rural Virginia took the daily edition of *The New York Herald-Tribune*. On many evenings, growing up, my parents took my sister Hallam and me to meet the 7:02 from New York as she slipped into the train station with low jangling bells followed by a grand whoosh of air brakes.

When the big canvas U. S. Mail bag was tossed off the mail car, my father and Ted Byrd, the man in charge of the depot at that hour, scurried over to retrieve it and safely drag it in from the tracks.

Working together with a pocket knife, they would slit the official post office seal, open the sack and rummage through everyone's mail until they found my father's *Herald-Tribune*. Then, after a stop at Haden's Frozen Custard on hot nights, we would go home and enjoy the newspaper on the same day it was published, not the next day when it would have been delivered by the Chatham post office.

I relished reading Jimmy Breslin, Suzy Knickerbocker, Art Buchwald and so many other innovative writers who contributed to that remarkable newspaper. Breslin's grace and style of reporting showed the power of being nose-to-nose with the people most basically affected by world-sized events—not the pinstripes pontificating over policy.

When I was fifteen, I sold my first newspaper story. It was about an old man in our neighborhood who had been the child of slaves during the Civil War. I went on my bicycle to interview him. *The Danville Register*, a local daily, bought and published the story. After that I was never far from the pen.

My big fork in the road came later, around 1966, after I had worked at several newspapers as an intern and on a full-time basis. I won a short story contest sponsored by the Southern Literary Festival, held that year at the University of Mississippi. The fiction judges were Robert Penn Warren, Peter Taylor and Eudora Welty. All three became cheerleaders for me as a writer, leading to a handsome grant from the Rockefeller Foundation to pursue fiction.

Others who gave me so much time and encouragement were Professor Evans Harrington at Ole Miss, as well as the literary agents, Robert and Susan Lescher, and Shannon Ravenel, then an editor at Houghton Mifflin and now a leading lady among editors of Southern fiction writing. I remain grateful for their efforts in trying to help me be a fiction writer.

So there before me lay the two roads—one luring me to try to make a living writing fiction with the support of serious literary luminaries, the other beckoning me to stick to what I knew for sure, reporting and writing. In the end, as I considered the unpredictable road of fiction writing, I could not see a way to marry and have a family with Margaret Nolting Williams, the extraordinary woman who became my wife.

Thus, I took the road to non-fiction and have made a living reporting and writing books and magazine articles. Early on, I helped start a weekly newspaper in New York City with my great friend Chris Hagedorn; it is satisfying that nearly fifty years later, *City News* continues to come out each week. From there, I moved on to Reader's Digest Magazine, at that time a powerful icon of Americana read around the globe in dozens of languages and editions.

Few writers have enjoyed such charmed years as I, traveling the country and the world and reaching millions of readers as Editor-at-Large for Reader's Digest Magazine. So, looking back, I am sure that as a young fellow I chose the right road. It all worked out. We raised our three children and now enjoy their company and that of six grandchildren.

But all along the way, in my spare time and for my own satisfaction, I worked on novels and short stories. Many of them are set in an imaginary town called Shaw's Pond in Southside Virginia. Unlike all of my professional writing, these stories are fictional.

What follows are a few of them, stories from the road not taken.

Henry Hurt.
Chatham, Virginia
July 17, 2016

I

Our Town: Legends of Shaw's Pond

S o you've never heard of Shaw's Pond. That's a wonder, considering all that's gone on here for thousands of years. Our people have only been here about 250 years, but during that short time we've hosted tragedies, scandals, mysteries and murders. We've seen political corruption, extortion, arson, rapes and serious fraud, not to mention debauchery, drunkenness and gross arrogance in high places. A few people have approached moral majesty in some arcane matter, but not often. And today most people are acting close to the way they always have. Not particularly good and not particularly bad, just trying to make a good run from birth to death, and then hoping to make the big leap to heaven.

Before our time, the Saponi Indians were the keepers of this ground. Earlier, scientists claim, people may have been here as long as ten thousand years ago, leaving sparse evidence of their lives. The Indians we know of did not leave written records, and when our people came, we learned little of their language. So there is no firm record, except for snatches noted by early explorers like John Lederer and, later, William Byrd. Yet, we can draw poignant clues about our predecessors from the exquisite little stone ghosts—in the form of pottery, game balls, spear and arrow points--that spring from the ground whenever a field is plowed or new land cleared or a garden turned.

For more than a century, we sanctioned slavery, which kept Negro people brought from Africa in a wretched bondage of both body and spirit.

Many white people did not like this system and said so, but most of those who owned slaves did nothing about it. It was simpler to let things alone, and not all that difficult to come up with crafty reasons to defend it. Then came the brutal War Between the States in which the only winner was America herself, perhaps justifying the whole five-year horror. Our people were terribly defeated. Among the treasures lost were our men and our money and, in some of the saddest cases, the very spirits of entire families. Following that, we suffered through a post-defeat occupation that drained away much of what was left, attracted vultures from the North to pick over the ruins, and nurtured hatred and meanness in the mildest of us.

Despite all this past excitement, most of the 1,700 people at Shaw's Pond today will tell you nothing ever happens here. Never did. It's almost as though if it happened at Shaw's Pond, down here in William Byrd County in Southern Virginia, it probably wasn't very important.

The thirty-acre natural pond from which we draw our name is a largely spring-fed body of fresh water, helped by a steady, slow-flowing creek. The pond has nourished life of some sort since the Triassic geological period when dinosaurs are said to have lolled about on its banks. Some believe that eons ago a meteorite crashed into the earth, spawning the unusual geologic circumstances that fostered the pond's creation.

But who knows what happened eons ago?

We do know that the pond is much deeper than any of the ravines and crevices and drop-offs dotted through this area. Its eastern end is nearly one hundred feet deep. Then it shallows up on the western end toward the mountains. Shaw's Creek comes into the pond from the west, after meandering down the mountains and through Bog Town. On the opposite end to the east, water runs out (we call the water flowing out of the pond Shaw's Creek, too) and wanders eastward until it runs into the Nolting River a few miles away. Down the line, the Nolting joins with other rivers, losing its name along the way. Eventually the waters flow into the Atlantic Ocean.

Our pond has always been one of nature's special gifts, an ever-present wellspring of life. Because of this pond our town has become the centerpiece of William Byrd County, and the mainstay of every living thing around it.

But before telling you more about Shaw's Pond, let me introduce myself. My name is Sam Cobbett. Actually, Sam Cato Cobbett, V. I am editor of

The William Byrd Tribune and live with my mother here in town. Much to my distress, my former wife and children live far away. My people have been around here for a long time, and I have some old family papers I think would help you understand what Shaw's Pond was like in the early days. For example, in 1823 my Great, Great, Great Grandmother, Mary Wilson Cato, came here from Lynchburg as the bride of William Cobbett. In her first letter home, a surviving treasure in our family, she offered her gratitude to her parents for the good life they had given her. She then described her first impressions of Shaw's Pond:

> *We arrived at the Cobbett house in the deep night, my new husband having insisted that we press on so he could get back to his office soon as he could in order to publish his newspaper on time. A late, low moon had helped show our way, and danced lightly on the pond when we reached the town. Since the pond lies in the front, we approached the house from the rear, unlike the approach to your house, or to the houses of our friends in the countryside where a long road leads up to the front and circles around. Mister Cobbett had been forthright in explaining how different things would be at Shaw's Pond where, as you know, his family has lived since well before Independence. A boy named Turnbop awaited us at the side entrance with a light and took the horses and carriage.*
>
> *We were received on that first night by an elderly servant named House John who showed us to a small supper in the morning room. After supper, we retired to our quarters. I was weary from our journey and all the wedding festivities in Lynchburg, and thus grateful to Mister Cobbett and his family for allowing us to have a quiet arrival. I hasten to say that I had a good feeling about the easy way Mister Cobbett spoke to both Turnbop and House John. But, with some apprehension, I realize those two Negroes are not the field hands about whose treatment we've heard the troubling reports.*
>
> *Next morning, soon after daybreak, I looked out of our front window and, through giant trees of poplar and oak, beheld a sight as wondrous as a pastoral scene in a lovely*

*painting. Our windows look south, across the pond around
which the town is established. On that first morning, a fluffy
mist hung over the pond, making it appear that we were looking
down upon the tops of the clouds. Soon enough, the sun's rays
pulled the mist upwards until it melded into the blue skies,
leaving a shimmering body of water so placid that the reflections
themselves looked like softly colored paintings. Beneath our
windows are the Cobbetts' gardens, eagerly blooming. Among
the yard fowl are majestic peacocks, themselves in bloom, who
seem to compete with the flowers for the sun's favor.*

*Only two houses stand on the north side of the pond—
that of the Cobbetts and that of the Shaws. Both face to the
south. Across the pond, as well as on the eastern and western
ends, stores and stables and smithies are along the way. I can
see two churches as well as the bank and the court house on
the eastern shore. Just down from the court house, the rear
of Mister Cobbett's newspaper office is in view, sitting a
hundred or so feet from the pond's shoreline.*

*As dawn lightens, I can see smoke rising from the chimneys
of some of these buildings. Mister Cobbett says that during
the cold weather, the smoke hugs the surface of the pond like
a tucked-in blanket. He worries that the town's increasingly
vigorous commerce is going to destroy the usefulness of the
pond if people are not restrained from dumping everything
they don't want into it.*

*He says that some people disagree and argue that everyone
should be able to use the pond as they choose. Others claim
that Mister Cobbett would not care at all except that his home
house stands on the edge of the pond. Such criticism does not
seem to ruffle Mister Cobbett in even the faintest way. Odd as
it seems, he appears to enjoy it! I believe he feels any controversy
makes his newspaper more interesting to its readers.*

*On the western end of the pond, out of clear sight of our
house, is the settlement called Bog Town where smoke rises from
two distilleries as well as from other enterprises and a number
of houses. Mister Cobbett believes that no one should be living*

there because of the threat of high water, soggy ground and the insect infestations he thinks are spawned by such conditions. Bog Town has attracted a low order of people, some of them leftover Indians, miscreants and even some half-breeds believed to be run-away slaves. As for the Indians, Mister Cobbett has a more tolerant view than most I've known who live this close to the frontier. He seems to think it would be better to have some of the Indians among us rather than driving them all off to the south and west. He's not sure that these ideas of giving them tracts of land to live on by themselves will work as well as some of our Government officials seem to think.

But what a piddling digression all of this is! What I am writing to tell you is that Shaw's Pond is so lovely and serene that I feel blessed to know I shall look out upon it every morning so long as I live here, which I pray will be for all my days. From my several visits into town, I find little of the rushing about that you have in Lynchburg. Instead, I find a tranquility that is pleasant and comforting as I adjust to my new life.

Mother, I know you worry that I have no close friends here. I want you to know that this beautiful pond itself seems to my mind like a friendly matron to whom I can turn, a lady of beauty and serenity who has been here longer than anyone, who has watched the Indians and all the people and creatures who have drawn their sustenance from her since the beginning. I think of her as a guardian angel set down here by our Heavenly Father to watch over one of His special little gardens of the world. In her surely reside answers to questions I would ask no one, and whether or not she answers me, I find her waters comforting as I begin my new life, earnestly wanting to be a good wife and praying for the blessing of children.

If you are still reading this, my dear Father, I want you as well as Mother to know how grateful I am for your compassionate patience with me, especially when you surely feared I would become an old maid. I will be forever grateful to you for not making me go husband-hunting at the Billing, Wooing and Cooing Society at the Springs, and you have my evermore appreciation for tolerating my studies and travels far beyond what might be expected. But now, perhaps more so due to my advanced years, I feel that I am ready for marriage and ready to make my life with Mister Cobbett. He is a most interesting and satisfying husband—thoughtful, tender, smart and surprisingly well read.

Grandmother Mary Wilson, who was 24 when she wrote this letter to her parents in 1823, went on in this vein for several more pages. As her long years at Shaw's Pond went by, she had a great deal more to say in her letters and journal. I give you these few words to provide an early and contemporaneous description of our little piece of the world.

Committed to embracing what was given her, my grandmother's affection for Shaw's Pond and its people never wavered as her strong heart kept beat with her times for one hundred and one years. An expansive reader and writer, her time on earth touched three centuries with the grace and quiet eloquence of a woman blessed with wisdom, as well as the greatness of years. Eventually, many of the Cato family's books came to our house, bringing us the riches of worlds we had never seen, telling us stories we had never heard and giving us thoughts we had never known.

And most of what I know dates back to 1823 with this grand woman's arrival at Shaw's Pond.

When I think of Shaw's pond before our settlers arrived, I see an Indian village in a tranquil setting with light smoke hanging low, the pungent smells of game cooking. Beaver and deer hides, as well as those of bear, are stretched around trees, curing for trade. Women and children are working in gardens of tobacco and vegetables. Men are fishing from canoes in the pond, as others return from the deep woods with game. Little bronze-skinned children with shiny black hair are at play as bare-breasted women go in and out of long houses made of straw and mud.

My image, of course, is a montage of stereotypes, since we don't have much to go on. We do know that in our part of the new country, no prolonged violent confrontations took place between us and the Indians. Mesmerized by our firewater and fire sticks, the Indians were docile for the most part as we shoved them relentlessly toward the less populated regions to the south and west. Still, sadly, our only image of this Indian village is the silent one in the mind's eye.

Yet, I suspect our Indians had a telling instinct as strong as that of Homer or Dickens, or even Grandmother Mary Wilson. But their medium was in the form of words spoken instead of written. If in fact the Indians did have such a telling instinct, it was muted by the sad hand fate dealt them. Here in Southern Virginia, we were in too big of a hurry to listen very carefully, or to pay much attention to their language, or to write down much of what we heard or even saw. But generations of us have marveled over their stone tools, pottery, adornments and weapons absorbed by our soil, elegant artifacts forever popping up like crocuses to instill awe and wonderment.

What we know for sure is that their thirty-acre body of water, called Indian Pond in the earliest references, became part of a land grant to Nathaniel Shaw, along with 5,500 acres, in 1758. By 1768, Nathaniel Shaw was parceling out lots around the pond and promoting it as a good site for a town bearing his name. Over the next decade, people put up houses and churches and store buildings and established various commercial enterprises such as a bank, livery stables, tanneries, a hotel, distilleries and doctoring establishments. Also, during that time, my own forebears established our newspaper, first called *The Shaw's Pond Tribune* and, later, *The William Byrd Tribune*.

By 1778, a village was laid out and chartered by the Virginia Legislature as Shaw's Pond and designated as the official seat of William Byrd County. First, the governor appointed magistrates; then the Legislature appointed a judge, an old man who happened to be Nathaniel Shaw's eldest son, to hold court. Constitutional offices were established, including that of a sheriff and a court clerk. A succession of county court houses and clerk's offices were built, each one a little more imposing than the last. The Town of Shaw's Pond set up its government and promptly began collecting taxes aimed to nurture the common welfare.

As you can see, my family has been around as long as any family but the Shaws. Yet, as my father often said, all of this was long ago and far away. It amused me to hear him say that, for it seemed to me that nothing about Shaw's Pond was long ago or far away. Many of the people have exactly the same names as their forebears. Many families, like ours, have been in the same house, or on the same land, for generations and have been in the same kind of work. For more generations than I can count, the Shorter Family has been in the mechanical repair business, having started out fixing wagons and carriages. Today, they work on cars. Old Doctor Greene at the pharmacy is operating in the same spot where his forebears ran an apothecary shop. Our family is still running the newspaper, and the Haymeses are still building roads and bridges. And, of course, countless families in the countryside are farming the same land as their families have farmed for generations.

And thanks to an agreeable Legislature in Richmond, the Shaws themselves still manage to keep one of their own roosting on the bench as judge in the Circuit Court of William Byrd County.

So, truth is, not much has changed at all.

As was true of our forebears, what people most enjoy here is talking and telling. And they talk and tell a lot. Not only do they talk to each other, they talk *about* each other. And they do so with affection, with humor, with sadness, sometimes with venom. Not infrequently, they will embellish their tales, but soon enough the embellishments become permanent adornments to whatever really happened. People especially enjoy secrets—telling them, hearing them, betraying them.

Because I was born here, I've known the people of Shaw's Pond all my life. I guess you could say I'm one of them. Having been around people who talk a lot, I'm comfortably acquainted with men and women who died long before I was born. One doesn't need to have been here in person to know what happened—or even to know who said what to whom. If you just stay quiet and listen, you can hear it all.

And, to keep the record straight, I haven't been here for all my years. Truth is, I lived away from Shaw's Pond for a total of eighteen years—four years (ages 18 to 22) away at college from 1963 until 1967; two years in the Army in Vietnam from 1967 until 1969, and then, later, between 1972 and 1984, a twelve-year absence when I was sent away after my father's death in 1972. Now there's a story that takes some explaining. People were deeply puzzled over why a man, in this case myself, would up and leave a good job with a family business at Shaw's Pond and move away. No one, however, was as initially shocked as I.

At the time of my father's early death, three years after I returned from Vietnam, I was happily working at the family newspaper alongside him and my grandfather. I had my eye on several young women, any one of whom might have made a good wife. I had never doubted that at my father's death, I would immediately take over the paper. But my grandfather, who was then in his mid-eighties and active at the paper and in every other way, had his own ideas. The afternoon following my father's funeral service, Grandfather took me into our house office, sat me down across from him at the huge family desk and came right to the point:

"Sam, your daddy should never have let you settle at home so young to start with," Grandfather told me. "You need to get away from here for a while. Get out of Virginia. Go learn some things we don't already know. Wouldn't hurt if you found yourself a wife and brought some fresh blood in here. When you have something to bring back to the table, come on home and you'll be welcome. It doesn't take a lot to run this paper, and we've got some good help. I'll run it just fine by myself."

That blunt directive shocked me, particularly coming from my grandfather, the man I most revered in the world at that moment. I also knew he meant what he said. A month later, I departed, found work as a reporter in Washington, and soon after that took a wife. I was away from Shaw's Pond from 1972 until 1984, the year my grandfather died in good health at the age of 95, soon after writing his own obituary. Only then did I go home to Shaw's Pond for good--to care for the newspaper as well as my mother. I also kept tabs on our dwindling farm operations that were mainly under lease, but also showing nice returns from myriad federal agricultural subsidies.

While I did not know whether, by Grandfather's standards, I had brought anything important to the family table, any such reservations evaporated on my first night back. Before we had even buried Grandfather, who was laid out in the big front hall, my mother handed me an envelope he had left for me. In his firm hand, on a piece of heavy white paper, he had written:

Sam:
Welcome home for good, I trust.
When everything is settled, I believe you will be confronted with sufficient opportunities and responsibilities to occupy yourself usefully for the rest of your years. I pray

*those years will be as long and as healthy and happy as my
own. You will find the combination to our main vault on a
slip of paper hidden beneath the matting that displays your
first arrowhead. Only you know the one I mean. In the main
vault, you will find other keys and combinations you will
need. Everything is clearly marked. I am glad to say that I
have no advice for you whatsoever. If I felt you needed advice,
I would not entrust you with so many of our family's earthly
treasures.*

*I do want you to know that I cherish the pleasure you
have given me over the years we've shared. I think of our
walks, our fishing, our arrowhead hunts, as well as our great
mutual enjoyment of reading and writing and talking. You
may be surprised to hear me say how deeply distressed I was to
send you away after your father's death, but it had to be done
and was the right thing to do. No one missed you more than I.*

*On another very important matter, I am profoundly
sorry your wife did not work out, but I could have predicted
that from the earliest days. She was thinking about what she
wanted, not what you needed and wanted. In fact, I think
down deep, she thought we were all crazy, so it's not surprising
that her mindset should incubate disaster in marriage. Even
if she could have understood your duties to the family and to
the newspaper, I do not think she would ever have devoted her
life to those interests. The greater tragedy is that your Little
Sam and Allie seem estranged from you, and unless you can
turn that around, then my hope is that you will find yourself
a new wife and start all over.*

*Meanwhile, I sense the Reaper is near. The dogs are
nervous. The peacocks are jumpy and crying at night. I've
always believed that I would know when He was ready for
me. I find nothing grim in His countenance and look forward
to my journey with Him across the wide water. And I expect
in time to welcome you into our Heavenly Father's home.
I'm tempted to tell you to keep your life in good order so that
you'll get there, but that would sound too much like advice.*

However, please know that in case you do make it, I will save you a nice mansion.

Affectionately,
Sam Cobbett, III
April, 1983

Six months after Grandfather's death, I had largely finished up my business in Washington and was back here at Shaw's Pond. It was wonderful to be home for good. Until my return, I did not realize how much I missed our town. At night, I'd walk around the streets, looking at the old buildings and houses and thinking about all that had gone on in them. These structures were like old friends to me—each with its own face, especially in the shape and style of the windows that like eyes looked out on the world. I also found myself savoring the words and faces of people I had not seen for so long, often recognizing in young men and women the eyes and stature of one of their parents I'd known long ago.

Whether or not I was living at Shaw's Pond may have been important to me, but certainly not to others. In fact, only the closest family friends seemed to be aware of my absence of twelve years. To show you what I mean, consider this: one afternoon, shortly before Grandfather sent me away, I was sitting around Junior Shorter's Garage talking and trading knives while my car was being worked on. An old fellow sitting there named James Osborne admired my wooden-handled pocketknife, looked at it and offered to trade me his small bone-handled two-blader. It suited me. Had I been told, I would not have believed that this trade would be the last time I ever swapped knives.

Then, one day after I had returned home, I was standing in the post office one morning going through my mail. Suddenly, beside me, I heard a faintly familiar voice:

"Sam, you never told me how you liked that little knife. Holdin' up okay? Feel right in your hand?" It was James Osborne, hands tucked in his pockets, leaning forward and looking down at his former knife that I was using to slit open the mail.

"It's doin' fine, James," I said, continuing to open envelopes. "Nice knife. How's my little wooden-handle doin', okay?"

11

"Naw, it broke right after we traded," James said. "That wooden part just come out, like it won't never put in there right. But that's awright. I'm glad one of us made out okay."

Then he was gone, around the corner to check his box. I can't be sure, but I believe old James Osborne simply believed he had not seen me around for a while and was unaware that I had been gone for twelve years.

So, as you can see, in some ways it doesn't matter whether you are here or not. If you are supposed to be here, well, you're here. And, I must say, my heart never left Shaw's Pond. Of course, I did make visits home, read our newspaper every week, carried on a good correspondence with my kinsmen and thus kept up pretty well with what was going on.

It might have been different if I had brought a family home, but my wife Alexandra had gotten fed up with me (and particularly disillusioned over everything she heard about Shaw's Pond) and taken off with our son, Sam VI, and our beautiful little girl, Alexandra Wilson, who we called Allie. My wife soon married a wealthy man in California, and I hardly heard from her again.

Under our divorce agreement, Sam and Allie were supposed to spend specified periods of time with me, but their mother had so poisoned them against Shaw's Pond that I doubted they would ever be willing to visit. This is a large sadness in my life, since I love our children and wish they could learn to enjoy their heritage. More than that, I need them. At the very least, I need Sam Cobbett VI. There's a lot that needs doing around here.

Like the men in my family before me, I keep two offices at Shaw's Pond, in addition to the house office where sits the huge walnut partners' desk we all use at home. Each man still has his own drawer in that desk for important papers, a drawer respected as his even after his death. The drawer for William Cobbett, the settler who first came to Shaw's Pond, is comfortably stuffed with papers of his wife, Mary Wilson Cato Cobbett.

As for our offices in town, both are in the old brick bank building; one office can be seen, the other not. The office facing Main Street is designed to attract people to come in and place ads in our newspaper, as well as to report news events and to purchase newspapers and Posted signs. We're glad to get news of any sort, and there's not much we won't print. We report crime and court news and sports and social events. We relish printing unusual wills. People bring in over-sized tomatoes and cucumbers or big fish, or even slain deer for us to see. Readers also have brought in large thrashing snakes, raccoons and occasionally a snarling bobcat. Our secretary makes a photograph of each trophy or curiosity and puts it in the paper. We're glad to see them all. And so are our readers.

As for my second office at the newspaper, it is behind the front office and out of sight. A heavy firewall separates the front and the back. The back office has no windows. And only I have the key.

Certainly plenty of the people I deal with know about our back office, but I rarely invite people here. I like it that way. A man without a refuge, without a sanctuary, can become a man without moorings. He's apt to lose his grip on things such as his marriage, his friendships, his drinking, even life itself. For me, it's a good place to go and think and even talk to myself about the things I read, the people I know, and all the news I hear up and down the streets of Shaw's Pond. Now and then, I bring people back here to talk, usually special people who have something to say, but I prefer to see them elsewhere.

In this second office is where we keep much of the family library. The floor-to-ceiling rows of shelves hold thousands of books, going back generations. Many of the books were brought here by Grandmother Mary Wilson, lots of them read and some re-read. Sometimes I wonder seriously if anyone in my family ever discarded a book. I can recall my father and my grandfather, who were otherwise sensible men, saying, "There's never been a book published that was a bad book." These two men were like children at a zoo, or in a museum of natural history, the way they would chortle with delight, or scorn, or something in between, whenever they came upon a new book. As for the books that ended up on the shelves of the back office, many were cherished almost as children or family dogs.

"What you see here is powerful evidence of the telling instinct," my grandfather used to say, waving his hand towards the shelves of books. "People just can't help telling. If they know something, the best part is to tell somebody—whether they're standing on the street jabbering or shut up somewhere scribbling." Clearly, our family has preferred the scribblers.

When I was a child, my grandfather, as well as my father, allowed me into the back office to read, but that's all. No playing, no poking around— just to read. On such occasions, it was up to me to announce the area I felt like reading in, such as, say, "Horses" or "Civil War" or "Indians" or

"Automobiles." After being asked a couple of questions about my specific interests, I would then be given a book considered suitably edifying on the stated subject, escorted to a reading chair and told to sit down and read. In our family, reading was serious business, not something to be wandered into and out of aimlessly.

Reading in bed was disdained, for that time was reserved for tending to one's wife, rogering her now and then, and sleeping. My people believed it was suitable to read history and philosophy and science during the daylight hours, but literature and poetry were to be enjoyed only in the evenings before bedtime or perhaps of a Sunday afternoon. For the women in the family, it was different. Being the privileged flavor, they could get away with reading what they pleased after the noon hour. In some of her letters and in her journal, Grandmother Mary Wilson explains that women deserved more latitude in their reading times because it left them less idle time in the afternoons for what she called "chatter and gossip."

On the rear wall of the back office is a fireplace that appears to have been put in where a door once stood. It has a coal grate, but I hardly ever use it since coal has become hard to find in these parts. I keep just enough on hand to start a fire on the most frigid of mornings. Then I go out for a little walk. I like this, since the coal smoke hangs low over the pond and the town and makes it smell like a time long ago.

Toward the rear of the back office is a good-sized walk-in vault that's been here at least one hundred and forty years, going back to Civil War times when this building was the Planter's Bank. I keep in the vault many of the same things my forebears kept: guns, extra good whiskey and brandy, extra good cigars and smoking tobacco, particularly valuable old books, gold coins, some financial records and, of course, certain treasures that should be shielded from prying eyes—treasures like the frayed old Daddy Book that keeps the facts straight on wayward husbands and wives and the actual lineage of their offspring. I also have some side meat and several cured hams hanging here as well. They are safe from thieves and keep the whole room smelling as it should—a nice blend of old leather books, smoked meat and cured tobacco.

I'm a lucky man to have at my fingertips so many cherished physical possessions. Sometimes I think I have too much for my own good. I'm not sure whether I am the custodian of these treasures, or they of me. But their care is my duty. I am the fifth man in a descending line to carry the same name, reaching back to 1824 when Grandmother Mary Wilson Cato Cobbett named her firstborn Sam Cato Cobbett. Sometimes I get confused about this, especially when I'm drinking whiskey, of which I have had a plenty. On foggy occasions, I sometimes wonder if I'm someone new, or if I'm merely the latest version of a 175-year-old model. Each possibility has its advantages—and its disadvantages.

When my wife, Alexandra, finally took the children and walked out on me for good, one of the last things she said speared my heart more searingly than I think she ever hoped. She did have a way of hitting things dead center--a characteristic I admired until facing it myself. "Sam," she said as a parting shot, her voice lilting in a way I once loved: "You know what your problem is, at least your *biggest* problem? You don't know who you are, or even what century you're living in. If you could have ever gotten just that much straight, we might have had a life together."

Now, I am not going to tell you she was wrong. Nor am I sure she was right. And I suppose this ambivalence goes to the heart of why I find it easiest to retreat to my duty, true to all that has gone before me, true to everything I know except, perhaps, myself.

Running our town's newspaper for six generations has given my family a pretty good perspective on Shaw's Pond and William Byrd County. In our pages, we have treasured and celebrated our natural beauty as well as the native intelligence and comic genius of our people. We have bragged about our history, our war heroes, and our beauty queens. We have tried hard to tell what has happened—all of it, both the good and the bad.

The challenge of getting at the truth and telling the public about it is more daunting than you might think. Any situation or individual is always so much more complex than what appears on the surface. The man who stands before you is, of course, an individual in the eyes of God and the law, but he is also a compendium of all that has gone before him—some of those things known and understood by him, others unknown and often unknowable. Just as in the case of an individual, a family is the sum of all those who have gone before—and the experiences of all those people.

All of this is true, too, of a town. And the voice of a newspaper should synthesize the seasons of a town's life from the time it started. Its pages, while still wet with ink, are reporting upon what instantly becomes the history of a place. Those pages, numbering into the thousands over the decades, become the final record of a town and its people. Such a repository of history is worthy of reverence.

In similar fashion, the fireplace of an ancient house invites enchantment because of the generations of people who have stared at the flames in that very space as they've done their thinking and talking and even their loving. Their shining eyes have stared at the very space where the flames still dance. The firebox sits as a flickering sanctuary of respect for all that its hearth has seen and heard. The space possesses the sanctity of a cathedral. So, like an ancient fireplace, or the banks of Shaw's Pond, our newspaper has been a canvas for the portrait of our town and our people since almost the beginning.

At its best, the newspaper is the sum of the wondrous, the sad, the evil, and the ugly. When the paper cheats on what's happening by glossing over something—just as when a family or an individual or a business cheats--distortion of the larger truth has been sparked, whether known by only one person or the entire community. Like little cancers, such distortions take root, grow, prosper and take on fresh sharpness to gnaw away at larger truths. Finally, when the whole is threatened by a sprawling, evil lie, few are aware of how such a point was reached--and those who know are no longer able to eradicate the damage, or even to stop what they have set in motion.

As for me, I concede that while living away from Shaw's Pond and working as a reporter, I picked up some habits that verged on lying, cheating and stealing—including trying to conceal my Southern Virginia accent when in high company, or trying to pretend to be someone I was not and in so doing betraying who I am. While I would never echo the purist's notion that such indulgences make me an absolute liar or a cheater or a stealer, I deeply agree with Doctor Ralph Stanley, the great musician who, upon returning to live and make music at his mountain home in Virginia, spoke of his weariness over having fallen into a life of "compromise and accommodation." In the end, the only way he knew to cure this malaise was to go home.

With the worldly knowledge I brought home to Shaw's Pond, I was certain I could sever the worst of the compromise and accommodation that had crept into my character. Here at Shaw's Pond I could restore my soul and become as noble as I believed my father and grandfather to have been, carrying forward the best in my forebears, including that remarkable woman who was really the founder of our family, Mary Wilson Cato Cobbett.

But, as I was to learn, nothing so lofty is ever so simple.

Now that you know something about Shaw's Pond and William Byrd County, let me tell you a few stories about some of the people I know here and some of the things that have happened to them. But doing this is tricky because most of them know me as well as I know them. That's where the balance lies, keeping me from telling too much lest they start telling about me.

Take Miss Kate Sims, a thrice-married octogenarian who held onto her maiden name decades before it was fashionable. Miss Kate and her life-long companion Emma could tell some tales on me, so I'll tread lightly in my accounts of them and their odd lives on an old tobacco plantation still called Bright Leaf.

As for the Chumbleys, they've always been friendly to me, but they are a rowdy bunch from the northern part of our county and seem often to alienate their neighbors. As a boy, I grew close to some of the older Chumbleys and learned to enjoy their persimmon wine, a concoction I've not met elsewhere. Since those old days, some of the Chumbleys have gone through school and, to be sure, Attorney Pickeral ("Pick") Chumbley is their pride and joy. He frequently serves as court-appointed counsel in cases at the William Byrd Courthouse, including an occasional dispute among Chumbleys themselves.

Or consider the Barksdale Family whose peculiarities and eccentricities have bemused us for generations as they jump from overalls to overalls with more frequency than some other families. And I want to tell you about the sad saga of poor old Dillard Grubb and the crafty but much beloved Preacher DeLano Hairston who got poor Dillard into the biggest mess of his life. And I would be remiss if I failed to tell you about the Karewskis—a strange bunch who, as you will see, changed my life forever. And, of course, the Jacksons who had a few good years on their way from overalls to overalls.

But let's get to the stories....

II

Mr. Karewski's Dancing Bear

S haken by weather and age, the rambling house where the Karewskis lived presided over nearly a block of Bog Town, a scrappy settlement just west of Shaw's Pond in Southside Virginia. Several generations of the Karewski family had lived there and were among the last townspeople to tend a big garden and to keep pigs, chickens, and a milk cow. To our knowledge, they were the only Karewskis in William Byrd County, or perhaps even in the whole Commonwealth of Virginia. They stayed to themselves, and did not go to church; rumor had it they were churchless Catholics.

On Thursdays, when I passed the house delivering newspapers, the Karewskis' dogs went wild, barking and snarling. Hulking gray-black animals that never smiled, they hurled themselves toward the road, jerked to violent stops by the chains that held them. I rarely saw anyone outside the Karewski house, but when I cut my eyes toward the upper windows, it sometimes seemed that someone was looking out at me. Sometimes, too, I heard music drifting from the house, either a piano or what I took to be a fiddle being played slowly like a violin. Around town, people said that earlier Karewskis had been traveling show people who worked in circuses and carnivals and had a stuffed bear--formerly a dancing bear--in their living room.

From my earliest years in grade school, I was intrigued by the little Karewski girls, Anna and Maria. They were both a little older than I and a grade ahead of me. Though in the same grade, Maria was a year or so older than Anna. So shy, they usually spoke only to each other. They said they were sisters, but nobody believed it--nor did it much matter. Anna had blue eyes and flaxen hair, while Maria's hair was black as wet coal and her eyes nearly as dark. Anna's hair was wild and tangled, as if unacquainted with a hairbrush, while Maria's fell straight and sleek, looking almost polished.

Some children brought their lunches to school while others were given lunch tickets bought by their parents, entitling them to eat in the lunchroom. Anna and Maria always brought their lunches in separate brown paper sacks. After lunch, they carefully folded first the wax paper that held their sandwiches and then the paper sacks and took them home to be used again the next day. Over time, the sacks had taken on the sheen of old leather.

I had a lunch ticket, but I sometimes asked my mother to fix me a lunch to take to school. She put my sandwich and apple in a tin lunch pail. Then, on my way to school, I would hide the lunch pail in the milk crate down by the road and put my lunch in the paper sack I kept stashed there for that purpose. At lunchtime, when we were allowed into the schoolyard, I looked for a spot not far from where Anna and Maria sat, hoping to become friendly with them. Thinking back, I suppose I was hoping they would become friendly with me.

Since neither girl seemed interested in me, now and then I'd sit nearby and look at a comic book. I enjoyed hearing them talk to each other. Their conversation was sprinkled with words and expressions I didn't know, so I was never sure what was being said. While I was enchanted by Anna's effervescent blonde hair, in the end Maria remained my favorite. Her black hair was so luxuriantly polished that I longed to rub it with the backs of my fingers, just to know how it felt. Now and then, it seemed, Maria glanced at me as if she was aware of my interest.

The girls had a sullen older brother, Joey, a large, strong boy who was in the eighth grade. No one had to tell me to stay out of his way. Other pupils teased him about his old clothes and funny shoes, and mimicked him relentlessly because he was tongue-tied. He often got into fights. Joey once sent a tormentor to the doctor for stitches to close a gash from a sharp rock. His parents were called in, and that was the first time I saw the pretty young woman people assumed to be the children's mother. We were just getting out for first recess, and I saw her up close in the corridor. She was small with olive skin, black hair, and luminous gray-green eyes that said nothing. Much younger than Mr. Karewski, she stood behind him with her chin at a slight upward tilt, hinting at an aloofness over the trouble at hand.

Joe Karewski, who owned and ran the cobbler's shop in Bog Town, was a heavy, muscular man, bristling with tension. He had bushy black hair and a wild beard. On that day, there in the corridor, his wide eyes constantly moved, searching others' eyes, seeking something, perhaps an unspoken insult that would start a fight. I sensed that even the teachers were afraid of him.

The Karewskis met with the principal in his office, the window of which was right above the playground. The only voice that came from the open window that day belonged to Mr. Karewski as he bellowed. When the confrontation was over, a few of us gathered to watch as the Karewskis left the building. Angry and humiliated, Joey clenched his fists at his sides as he stomped out of the school. He and the woman followed Mr. Karewski toward their large old station wagon parked on the street near the playground.

"*Ya goddamn hog-grubber!*" Mr. Karewski yelled at Joey, swatting at the boy and pushing him into the back seat. The woman silently took the front seat and looked straight ahead.

Once the doors were shut, Mr. Karewski twisted around and began beating his son. I could see his big arm flailing a strap up and down—not just a few whacks, but a beating that probably went on for a full minute. Those of us who had scurried over to gawk could hear Joey's screams. I never knew exactly what happened after that, but Joey never came back to school and went to work fixing tires at Otey Crider's gas station and working at the family's shoe shop.

I was forbidden by my parents to enter Mr. Karewski's cobbler's shop to peddle newspapers, so I usually glanced in when I passed and sometimes glimpsed him scowling over his work. The few times I was in his presence at the post office or when he came in to renew his small newspaper ad, his language was seasoned with angry, harsh-sounding phrases such as *stampers*, his word for shoes. Or I think of the time he yelled at my friend Coleman over some minor affront and called him a goddamn *hog-grubber*.

Within our family, my grandfather liked to call our newspaper the *Yelper*, echoing one of Mr. Karewski's references to it.

I was not privy to some of my parents' adult talk about the Karewskis, perhaps because Anna and Maria were my schoolmates. But I heard plenty about them on the street. Big Jim at the diner claimed that the young woman in the house was not the children's mother at all—that she, like the two little girls, had been stolen, in her case as a teen-ager. Big Jim also said that Joe Karewski had murdered his wife long ago and buried her in his vegetable garden. He said young Joey was Karewski's only natural child.

Up Main Street at the barbershop, White Willie claimed the Karewskis had a pet bear and that a crazy old lady, believed to be Joe's mother, a music-maker from their circus days, also lived in the house. He claimed the younger woman was actually the mother of little Maria and that Joe Karewski had stolen both mother and baby daughter during times when the family was gone for months on end with their traveling circus act. Like Big Jim, White Willie claimed the woman was in her teens when she first showed up at Bog Town with her baby.

Sometimes I enjoyed believing these stories and their variations, but it was hard to imagine that they could all be true. But, of course, I relished thinking that some or all of the stories *could* be true. Whatever the facts, each new purported detail about the Karewskis sharpened my interest in my two classmates as an inviting contrast to my own neat and orderly life.

No matter how harsh the rumors, my mother faithfully took our stampers to Mr. Karewski for repair, and I looked for chances to go into the shop with her. A glaring light hung over Mr. Karewski's workbench, but otherwise the lighting was dim, the murkiness infused with the smell of oil and leather. Mother's cheerful chitchat with Mr. Karewski was not returned in kind but with his nodded grunts of agreement. Sometimes we saw Joey or one of the girls in the rear of the shop, or the woman we took to be their mother. But they had nothing to say.

The only color in the place was a dusty calendar, long out of date, from AAA Auto Parts in Big Lick, showing a nearly naked bathing beauty. She smiled down at customers as they paid their shoe repair charges. My mother seemed not to notice the bathing beauty, and I tried to be discreet as I studied the image.

Then, about the time I turned ten and was in the fourth grade, I had a first-hand glimpse of the darkness of the Karewski girls' lives at home. It was after school on a murky, cold winter day, a Friday. My mother, in a huff over my carelessness, had driven me back to school to collect my coat I'd left on the rack in the classroom. The school was supposedly empty except for Mr. Meadows, who was somewhere in the basement, preparing to turn down the heat and turn off the lights before locking the building for the weekend.

When I entered my classroom on the first floor, a little awed by the quiet majesty of the big room's emptiness, I saw Anna and Maria huddled at a desk in a rear corner. Startled, they looked up at me. Their normally bright pretty faces were clouded with fear. Anna was crying, while the older Maria tried to comfort her.

"Y'all miss the bus?" I called out. Maria squeezed Anna, rocking her, and did not answer me. "My momma's here," I said. "She can take you home."

"*No!*" Anna called out, her sobs pulsing through her like electric current. "I'm *not* going home! I'll *never* go home again!"

Maria, more composed, but her eyes gleaming with tears, looked up at me. "Please go away," she said, shaking her head. "Anna will be okay, you just go away. Please leave us alone." She looked down at Anna and kept hugging and rocking her.

"But my mother's right here, just outside, and she can help you, drive you home…."

"*No!*" Maria shouted, leaping up and charging the length of the room and shoving me toward the doorway. "*Get out! Leave us alone!*" She pushed me into the corridor and slammed the door shut.

Back at the car, Mother spoke before I could say anything and was disgusted that I had managed to forget my coat for a second time.

"This is *ridiculous!*" she said. "You stay here and I'll get the coat." I protested by grabbing her hand and trying to tell her what had just happened, but she didn't want to hear anything from me. She slammed the car door and headed for the school.

Mother was gone for a long time. Just as I was thinking of going into the school to investigate, a car came into the parking lot and two official-looking women got out and went inside the school. A few minutes later, they came out with Anna and Maria, who were still holding each other and crying. The women ushered the girls into their car and drove them away. Then my mother returned to our car, clearly upset: "You weren't going to tell me about the little Karewski girls, were you?"

"Yessum, I was about to tell you, but you got after me about the coat before I could say anything. What's wrong with Anna and Maria? Who were those ladies they went off with?"

"They're from social services," Mother said. "Mister Meadows and I called them. It's all very sad and scary."

"What's scary?" I said.

"I think their father must be a very mean man, an awful man, and the girls are afraid of him and don't want to go home."

"I don't blame 'em. You shoulda seen Mister Karewski beatin' up Joey that day," I said. "What's social services?"

"They try to figure out how to help the children," Mother said. "But there's probably not much they can do."

"I don't blame 'em for not messing with Mister Karewski," I said.

"That's not the point," Mother said. "If the girls refuse to say what their father has done to them, nobody can do anything about it. They just have to go back home with him. And these poor children are not going to say a bad word about their father. They were terrified about us calling social services to help them."

"If they're smart, those old ladies will stay out of his way," I said.

Then, as if turning a page, Mother calmly switched on the interior lights of the car, braced her hands on the steering wheel, turned and looked at me intently: "Sam Cobbett, I don't want you *ever, ever* under *any* circumstances, to have *any*thing to do with the Karewskis. You are not to go to their shoe shop by yourself, and certainly not to their house. You can be polite, but absolutely nothing more. Is that clear?"

"Yessum," I said. "Where's my coat?"

"I forgot it," she said gruffly and headed the car toward home.

After that strange encounter, the girls seemed different to me, perhaps because they knew I had stepped for a moment into a secret compartment of their lives. As always, they stuck together at school, brought their lunches in mellow sacks and smiled and spoke if we happened to come face to face.

I still yearned to run my fingers along the back of Maria's glossy black hair. But it was different, no doubt because they knew that I knew what I knew.

That spring I became a pretty good baseball player, mainly a hitter and runner and became a regular on the team sponsored by Big Jim's Diner. The highlight came the day we went to Lynchburg on a bus for an exhibition game by the New York Yankees. We got to see Phil Rizzuto, Yogi Berra and the great Mickey Mantle. Just being in their presence heightened the thrill of playing for the rest of the season.

When summer came, I barely escaped being forced to go to a boys' camp in North Carolina, by pleading that I needed to play ball in the evenings and work around the family's newspaper so I could start learning the business. That gave me nice mornings on the streets and afternoons with my grandfather, exploring the verdant territory of William Byrd County. He and I crisscrossed the countryside as he showed me fishing spots, beaver ponds and old houses whose occupants were long gone, and even places where people had been murdered. He showed me the best places to find Indian artifacts on the hills overlooking the Nolting River. It was a good summer.

The Karewski girls hardly crossed my mind until school started up in the fall. They were back for the sixth grade with their odd charms, but different in mildly grown-up ways. While little Anna seemed paler and scrawnier than ever, Maria had filled out and was showing promising signs of breasts.

Then one day on the playground, I was eating my lunch with Coleman and another boy I played ball with. That's when Maria confidently called over to me: "Sam, how come you don't ever sit and talk to us?" She was smiling and looking at me, awaiting an answer. Her hair gleamed in the sunshine. My pals, sniggering, departed quickly.

"What?" I said, my voice croaking. "What do you mean? I mean, I talk. Y'all live at Bog Town, don't you? It's on my paper route."

"You wanna cookie?" she said. Now the other girl, Anna, was giggling. I went over to where they were sitting on a low concrete wall. Maria handed me a large peanut butter cookie.

"Thank you," I said. "My momma didn't send cookies in my lunch. She gives me a apple." I took a bite of the cookie. It was buttery and crunchy.

"But you get a lunch ticket," Maria said. "Sometimes you use it, and sometimes you bring your lunch out here and sit over there and listen to us." I flushed as both girls chuckled.

"Why'd I wanna listen to y'all?" I said. "I just like to sit out here." Maria was leaning toward me, grinning playfully. Her dark eyes had a way of smiling, too. I felt a pleasant little shiver of pleasure. At thirteen, she seemed so much older than me at eleven. We talked about peanut butter cookies, the merits of crunchy and soft. More immediately, we discussed a doodle-bug that was churning the dusty earth at our feet, and I told the girls about seeing a bobcat when I was walking in the woods with my grandfather.

"Do you know about our bear?" Maria asked. "Mishka, we had him when he was alive, too, and my poppa's poppa liked him so much he stuffed him when he died."

"Yeah, I heard about that bear. How come y'all have a bear?"

"Poppa and them used to be in the circus, and Mishka was the dancin' bear, and he danced when Poppa's momma made music for him," Maria said. She then fell quiet for a moment. "Some people think somethin's wrong with us because we worked on the circus." Maria's face darkened a little. She waited for me to comment.

"I don't know who thinks that," I said.

"What do *you* think?" Anna piped up. "People think we're funny just because we were circus people." Her blue eyes were on me. She too wanted an answer.

"Dunno, I don't know what I think. I mean, I think it's good, I mean, you know, not many people get to work in a circus. I think it'd be fun. Why're you asking me..."

Anna interrupted sharply, her tone accusatory: "Your momma and daddy are s-o-o-o-o rich and they tell you not to have anything to do with us, don't they?"

"They do not tell me that," I said.

"Why do you take the paper to everybody in Bog Town and skip our house and Poppa's shop?" Anna said. She was scowling at me, her pale little face pinched in the sunlight.

"I don't mean to," I lied again. The girls chuckled smugly, as though they had set a little trap and caught a mouse.

"Poppa was really pissed off last winter when you and your momma got them social ladies after him," Anna said. "Made a lot of trouble for us, and Poppa had to pay a lawyer to get it straight."

"*Stop* it!" Maria said, swatting her hand at Anna. "You know you better not be talkin' about that stuff."

"Hell," I said, emboldened by Anna's colorful language, "All my momma did was to want to give you all a ride home from school."

"Yeah, but we know she called those people that night and that was really dumb, Dumb's momma," Anna said. "More people try to mess with Poppa, the meaner he gets, and don't you go and tell your momma I said that!"

"I don't tell my momma nothin'," I said. "I didn't even tell her you all were in the classroom that night."

"Poppa said you did!" declared Anna, as if that settled the matter. "And he said you and your momma was meddlin' where you didn't have no business meddlin' and then them social ladies tried to make me and Maria tell lies about Poppa."

"Shut up, Anna," Maria said. "You better shut up about all that." It was clear to me that my mother and the social workers had brought hard times on the Karewski girls by trying to help them.

"What were you sayin' about that old bear, what's his name?" I said to Maria.

"Mishka," she said. "You oughta come see him."

"You let people come see the bear?" I said.

"It's Poppa's bear," Maria said. "And he lets people come see him sometime."

Then Anna chimed in: "But you'd be scared of the bear anyway. A lot of people are scared of Mishka."

"Why would anyone be scared?" I said. "The bear's dead and stuffed."

"You think you wouldn't be scared, but when Poppa gets kids to come look at Mishka they always get pretty scared," Anna said.

"I wouldn't be scared of any stuffed animal," I said. "Can I come over and see him?"

Sudden silence. The girls' eyes locked on each other. I wondered whether this whole conversation had been leading up to my asking to see the bear. I had an odd feeling. Then Maria's face clouded. "I don't know," she said. "Poppa's funny about who he lets see the bear. Sometimes he has a temper when somebody comes over, and then sometimes he's nice. Maybe you better not."

"Why does he have to know?" I said confidently. Instantly, a chill ran through me as I thought about what my parents would say and about what I had seen of Mr. Karewski. "Maybe if I come it would be better if he didn't know," I said.

"It dudn't matter," Maria said. "Your people wouldn't let you come over anyway."

"They won't know," I said with an added confidence, feeling a flicker of fear as I spoke.

A few days later, Maria told me that she had checked out things at home. She said her father was going out of town to Big Lick on Thursday, and that I could come to their house that afternoon to see the bear. The more I had thought about what I was doing—defying my parents as well as my fear of Mr. Karewski—the more uneasy I became. I even wondered if somehow I was being set up. But now I was stuck.

"What about your dogs," I said.

"Long as you stay on the path, they can't get you," Anna said. "The chains stop 'em right before the path."

Thursday came two days later. I had told no one about my upcoming visit. My fear of being caught by my parents competed with my fear of Mr. Karewski, even though he would not be there for my visit. And I'd found myself with a nice feeling about the sudden friendliness of the Karewski girls—at least Maria, who would soon have breasts like the older girls. My friend Coleman had brought a picture to school of a completely naked woman--breasts, pubic hair and all--and Maria stirred the same feelings in me that I had looking at the picture. In truth, my interest was as much in becoming friendlier with the Karewski girls--at least with Maria--as it was in seeing the stuffed bear.

Rain was falling lightly but steadily when I walked from school to the office to pick up my newspapers. I often went there after school anyway, whether I had papers to deliver or not. Occasionally I was given little reporting assignments that I enjoyed. My family had started *The William Byrd Tribune* when Shaw's Pond was established in the early 1800's. Every editor but the founder had been named Sam Cobbett--more precisely, Sam

Cato Cobbett. As that was my name, too, I was spared wondering what I would do for a living when I grew up.

On this day, I had a plastic sheet to put over my canvas bag of papers, as well as an ancient, abandoned raincoat, dirty and way too big for me that had been around the office all my life. As I got ready to go out, my father was in the back office, and my grandfather was standing behind the counter.

"Why don't you wait until it stops raining?" Grandfather said. "It's supposed to let up."

"I reckon I'll go on," I said.

"Keep your nose clean," he said, smiling. "Don't go hangin' around Jim's Diner, or foolin' around over at Bog Town," he added, still grinning.

His comment stopped me for a moment. Did he know something he wasn't telling me?

"No, sir," I said, unable to remember whether this was something he said to me every Thursday. Since he was smiling, I assumed he meant nothing unusual, and I went on my way.

Shaw's Pond in the rain is a wondrous place. There's something about the way the streets and sidewalks are laid out in relation to the pond. Like crooked roads coming from all directions, little rivulets dart toward the pond. As the rain continues, they join together in a great wash, carrying every small thing that can float. And the pond itself seems to change clothes during a rain, especially in the hot summertime when the steam rises and cloaks the water, the cooler rainwater hitting the surface. At times you can't even see across the pond, and then, a few minutes later, the view becomes fresh and clear. I like to stand near the street gutters and watch the downspouts from the old buildings create gushing streams, cascading through the streets, rushing to find their way to the pond.

So, on this day, I made my rounds in the rain, dropping papers off at stores and houses. I would return on Saturday to make my collections. As usual, I delivered the paper to Big Jim at Jim's Diner by handing it into the little window at the end of the streetcar through which he served black customers he considered unfit to come into the colored seating section of his diner.

"Awright, Sam!" Big Jim exclaimed jovially, taking his paper through the window. "Better be some fuckin' news worth readin' in here, and better not be nothin' about my ass."

"Yessir," I said. "Nothin' about you I heard about." Long ago, Jim had often appeared in our paper, once when he was convicted of murder and sent to prison, and for countless incidents of being drunk and disorderly. An outsider might have thought he was drunk this day, but I knew it was just Big Jim.

"Here, Boy!" he hollered at me as I started away. "Take this hat! You look like a goddamn fool walkin' around in the rain without a hat." Jim thrust a grimy baseball cap through the window. On the front were printed the words JIM'S DINER. "I grabbed it off a nigger's head come by here yesterday evenin'. I don't want no nigger walkin' around wearin' a hat with 'Jim's Diner' on it. You take it on with you and wear it."

"Yessir, Jim," I said. The hat smelled like chain saw oil and stale cooking grease. I put it on. "I gotta go now," I said heading up the street through the rain.

When I got to the west end of the pond and started into Bog Town, the road was flooded, but the cars and trucks were getting through. I passed Joe Karewski's shoe shop and glimpsed young Joey talking to a customer. I brightened at the thought that neither Joey nor his father would be at home, assuring a more pleasant visit with Anna and Maria and the stuffed bear.

Before me, shrouded in mist and rain, stood the Karewski's once-proud old house, its grayish paint peeling, the porch columns rotted at their bases. The elaborate Victorian flourishes in the cornices had crumbled at their edges. An elegant little second-floor balcony hung over the porch—a pathetic reminder of the house's grander days. It sagged above the wide front door, barely clinging to the house. A handsomely forged iron fence, now bent and rusted, ran along the sidewalk. Black walnut trees stood near the rambling structure, water gushing off its gutterless roof. The only sign of warmth, or life, was a light burning in an upstairs hallway beyond the little balcony.

I paused at the gate and tucked my newspapers into the canvas bag to keep them dry. The only sound was the rain until my hand moved the latch of the gate. The rusty hinge issued a sharp metallic screech. Dogs with wide heads, heavy necks and small hindquarters erupted from under the house and rushed toward me. They snarled and barked and slid in the mud. But I quickly saw that what the girls had told me was true. Despite

30

their straining, the dogs could not quite reach the pathway, their paws slicing into the muddy earth.

With the outburst from the dogs heralding my arrival, I felt sure that eyes were on me from behind the windows. I tried to appear calm and fearless as I walked out of reach of the dogs onto the porch. Even before I could knock, the double-front doors flew open. Standing there was neither Anna nor Maria--but Joe Karewski himself. Peering through his wild hair and beard, his face had its normal scowl. His belly pushed through a red flannel shirt and hung over his belt. In a calm voice and with a grim little smile, he said, "Aaaah, little Sammy Cobbett has come for a visit! The girls said you want to see our bear Mishka." He took firm hold of my upper left arm and pulled me toward him.

"Yessir," I said. Whatever confidence I'd felt a moment earlier evaporated.

"We were worried you would not come in the rain. I have a big towel here to rub you dry and then I will show you our Mishka." Keeping his grip on my left arm, he stood aside and held the screen door open so I could pass. I squeezed by the bulk of his body and his meaty forearm that held the door open, noting the stench of stale tobacco and fresh alcohol. I entered a dark and spacious front hall with a broad staircase in the front and a large room on the right. The door to the room on the left was shut. Other rooms were back past the staircase. A peculiar odor, a smell new to me, hung in the air. It was like sweet pipe tobacco, but much heavier. I must have shown a reaction to it, for Mr. Karewski put his head close and said, "Makes your smeller twitch, don't it?" He stared into my eyes.

"Yessir, but are Maria and Anna here?" I said, trying to keep my voice steady.

"You look surprised to see me," he said with a snort of laughter. "The girls tell me everything, and they will join us soon enough," he said. "First, let's get you all dried off, and then we will talk." As he spoke, he used the towel to rub my face and head vigorously, knocking off the Jim's Diner hat.

"Would you like to take off your shirt and pants?" he asked.

"No sir," I said. "I don't mind being wet."

His hand rested on my shoulder as he maneuvered me into the dimly lit room on the right. "Then we'll sit in the parlor while you dry off." He turned on a table lamp, and the light swept over a room that seemed, above all, heavy. The furniture looked big and prickly. The full-length velvet-like draperies were a dark purple, as if they had been fashioned from an old stage curtain in a theater.

He shoved me into a large brown armchair that swallowed me. My feet barely touched the floor. Mr. Karewski sat a foot away in another heavy armchair, near a small table. Up close, he was powerfully built with quick movements, and my mind's eye went to the image of him beating the daylights out of his son, Joey. I also thought of the terror I had seen in Anna and Maria the day I found them cowering in the classroom. My stomach muscles were clenched, and my throat felt like I couldn't swallow.

"What do you want to drink?" he said. "A little beer? Or maybe some wine?"

"No, thank you." The words squeaked out. I struggled to keep my composure. "Can I please see the bear now? I need to finish delivering my papers."

"No hurry, Little Sammy," he said, leaning toward me, offering a sly smile that revealed yellowing, crooked teeth. His florid tongue licked his red, raw-looking lips. "Me and the girls have wanted you to visit us ever since your momma sent the two cunts here to meddle in our business," he said in a measured voice. Then he bellowed: *"Cunts! Goddamned lying cunts! I had to hire that goddamned Pickle Chumbley to get 'em off my fuckin' back!"*

Then, gently, cunningly, he added, "But that's not all your fault, is it? It's your *goddamned Mother!"*

He sat back in his chair and belched. "So I don't be mad at you, and that's why I like for you to come here so we can have a little party with my girls. Do you wish we had invited your mother? Would your momma like to see Mishka?"

"I don't know," I nearly whispered as my voice had faded away. "I just came to see the bear." It was dawning on me that Mr. Karewski had, without doubt, made the girls lure me into this.

"Don't worry, Sammy, you'll meet our Mishka soon enough, and the girls and I want to have one of our little parties while you're here." Mr. Karewski sat back; his hands were now folded across his belly, and he looked at me with a faint smile that said, *I've gotchew!* I was sliding from my world into his and found myself, deep inside, trying to cling to my world. Then, leaning his face close to mine, he said, "Why did you not tell your people you were coming to see us today?"

"I don't know," I whispered, shrugging my shoulders. "I just didn't."

"You wanted to play with my little girls, didn't you?" he said smugly. "All by yourself." I didn't answer. "Let me bring your newspapers inside from the porch," he said, getting up. "We wouldn't want the rain to blow in on them and spoil them, would we? Or somebody like your momma drive by and see them and know you're here?"

As he got up, I realized I was about to vomit. The moment he cleared the room and I heard the front door open, I slid from the chair and went to the hallway door, hoping to find another way out. But my way was blocked by a tiny old woman standing there, no taller than my chin, staring up at me quizzically. She said nothing, but I could tell she was wondering who I was and why I was there. As I started to speak, she said in a heavy accent I could hardly understand:

"I heard voices...Oh God!" she exclaimed. "You're one of Joe's little friends! Child, you better run now! Oh God! Help us, help us!" She was shaking her head just as Mr. Karewski returned, swearing harshly at her in a strange language. The volume and force of his voice drove her backward into the hallway and out of my sight.

Then he turned back to me, again gripping my upper arm. "While I was outside I let all the dogs off their chains," he said. "I like for them to have a little freedom every day, so I let them run around the yard. Don't you think everything deserves a little freedom now and then?"

"Yessir, but I need to go," I said, wondering how, if I escaped, I would get by the dogs.

"And I want you to have something nice, too," he said, steadily pushing me back to the big chair and into it. "Now and then, little boys and girls need a special treat, just like the dogs, you think?" His face was close to mine. Under the stench of stale tobacco smoke, he smelled like freshly polished shoes. His dark eyes watched me from beneath thick brows. His tight smile made me think of a coiled serpent. "I think you deserve somethin' real nice at our party, and I bet you'd like to see Maria's little new titties, no? If you ask her real nice, she'll let you touch 'em."

"No sir, I don't," I said in a whisper. My lips were trembling. "I really don't."

"Oh, but Maria tells me she likes you, and that she has seen you look at her titties. I know she would like to let you see 'em up close," he said cunningly, clumping his thick hands together. "The party'll be fun, but I wish you'd brought your mother, since she likes sticking her nose in other people's business. But maybe she wouldn't like it, would she?" He shook his head sadly.

"No sir, she wouldn't."

"And we don't want your poppa or your grandfather to know either, now do we?"

"No sir."

"Don't worry, because your secrets are safe here. Grown-ups never know what happens in my house because no one who leaves ever tells. And that's how we make good friends with nice little boys like you." Somewhere upstairs, I heard the screaming of a bird, as if someone was plucking its feathers.

At that moment, seemingly on cue with the screaming bird, a powerful blast of thunder and lightning shook the house. The lights blinked and then went out. Just as my thoughts jumped to running away, a hand clamped around my right thigh, and I could feel the sour stink of Mr. Karewski's breath in my face. He kissed me on my right cheek, not an inch from my mouth, his harsh whiskers scraping my face. My cheek was wet with the slobber from his meaty lips.

Don't worry about the lights," he said, pulling away. "We have lamps and candles." Almost immediately, he struck a match and lit a candle on the table near where we sat. Feeble shadows danced briefly. "Now, I hope our little girls are okay in this storm," he said. "Should we start the party?"

"I don't know," I said. My throat was tight and I could hardly speak. I felt dizzy and nauseous. The bird was screaming. Mr. Karewski lit a cigarette.

"Which little girl do you like best?" he said. "Which one do you want to play with today?" He inhaled deeply and smoke poured through the thick crop of hair that filled his nostrils. Warming to his own question, he added, "I like Anna the best. I like her blonde hair and those big blue eyes. She's a little beauty, and it won't be long before she has some titties. Which little girl do you like best?"

"Both of 'em," I mumbled.

Mr. Karewski belched loudly, tapped his chest as if remedying his distress, and picked up a large pair of brass cymbals I had not seen from the floor by his chair. He stood up and clanged them together with all his might, thrusting them into the air with the verve of a circus ring-master. The sound ricocheted through the house. The bird screamed upstairs. Outside, the dogs erupted. Looking down at me, he slammed the cymbals together again and intoned in a grandiose voice:

"Ladeees and gentlemen, and children of all ages, we bring you the greatest show on earth, the freshest talent from the Land of Nod...I preesent *Anna and Maria!*" He dropped the cymbals and began clapping wildly. I had not moved, and he smacked my face with the back of his hand and yelled, "*Clap*, you little hog-grubber!"

As I started clapping, I saw Anna and Maria emerge from the dark recesses of the parlor. They had been there the whole time, I guessed, waiting to make this grand entrance. They were dressed in ballet costumes—Maria in white and Anna in a royal blue. Maria shot me a glance, but Anna seemed nearly catatonic.

"Let the show begin!" roared Mr. Karewski.

The girls were now in front of us, their skin caked in mascara and lipstick, faces shadowed in shame. Neither looked at me. Stoic, her mouth tightly set, Maria's eyes were filled with tears, but not a teardrop dared to flow down her face. "Now I want you to smile and come and sit on Poppa's knee." Each child took a seat on one of Mr. Karewski's knees. His hands around their midsections, he nuzzled each of them. "Now girls, I want you to talk to our company."

"Hi Sam," Maria said. She looked in my direction but not at me. I tried to say something but no words passed my lips. Anna sat silently as Mr. Karewski ran his fingers through her hair.

"Maria, Sammy tells me he wants to see your little titties." He tweaked one of her breasts. "You'll have to take your top off for Sam, like a good girl."

I looked away and slumped deeper into the chair. A rational thought crept through my terror: While I would like to see a real breast someday, I would never want to see Maria's. She must have hesitated, for Mr. Karewski next said, "You girls are very shy today. I think we should go down to the playroom and have a little wine, don't you think, Anna?" She said nothing.

"Now come, Anna, give Poppa a sweet kiss." With her eyes shut, she leaned forward and kissed him on his red raw lips.

"Now!" Mr. Karewski barked, rising up and dumping the girls onto the floor. "Before we go to our playroom, let's take Sammy to see Mishka the Dancing Bear." He clamped his hand around my upper arm and pulled me out of the chair. He ordered the girls to lead the way out of the parlor and across the hall.

The power was still off, but our eyes had adjusted to the dimness and we could see fairly well. As we moved across the front hall toward the closed door, the bird upstairs resumed its piercing screams. I thought about trying to jerk away and flee out the front door, but I knew the loose dogs would savage me. Just as I had this thought, Mr. Karewski stepped over and slid the dead bolt on the front door.

Maria opened the door across the hallway. On the far side of the room, near a window, stood Mishka, his front paws raised Pope-like before him. He was a few inches taller than I. His head turned slightly to his left in our direction; his mouth opened in a sort of smile. Mr. Karewski clamped his hand around my wrist as he pulled me across the room.

A faded red collar adorned with bells circled the bear's neck, and its left paw was punched through the skin of a dusty tambourine. Patches of brown fur were missing along the torso. The glitter of the glass eyes was dimmed by dust.

"Mishka came across the water with us when my grandpoppa came," Mr. Karewski said. "He worked with us in the circus and in Pennsylvania, and then we traveled the country with him. He was very old when I was a little boy, but I saw him dance."

It was then, as I stared at the bear, that something happened inside me, and I knew that whatever the risks of trying to run—savage dogs or being beaten or whatever—those risks were more tolerable than whatever was going to happen if we went to the basement.

"Come and touch him," Mr. Karewski said. "He likes that."

I reached up and touched the bear's dry black snout. "But why didn't he have any teeth?" I said, actually surprised to be asking such a rational question.

"Oh, he has a few in the back," said Mr. Karewski. "But Poppa pulled out his teeth when he was taught to dance. You see, we couldn't have him eatin' the little children who came to play with him and see him dance. Sometimes he would dance with the little children. I wish he could dance with you today, but he can't because he's dead."

"But he's too tall for a little child to dance with," I said.

"Shut up!" he yelled at me. "Mishka *always* danced with children!" With that, Mr. Karewski squeezed my upper arm harshly and yielded a faint smile. He knew that I would bolt if I could.

"I have to go now, or they'll wonder where I am," I said.

"But not yet, Sammy. He moved his hand to my shoulder, his thumb and forefinger against my neck. He gave me a hard, painful pinch. His mouth was opened slightly, like the bear's, his gums redder than his lips. "Come close, Maria, and let Sammy see one of your titties." She came to him, her eyes dull and dead, and her arms hanging at her sides.

"You show him, Poppa," she said.

Just as Mr. Karewski reached toward her, I wrenched loose from his grip and exploded toward the front door, as if stealing home from third. He was on me with the speed of a striking snake, blocking my way and lunging for me with both hands. I turned and shoved with all my might, pushing him off balance, and before I even thought about it, I was in the hallway and bounding up the staircase.

As I reached the top of the stairs, it was almost dark, and the great bird commenced its screaming, now with a harsh flapping of wings. I turned to the left and ran along the banister toward the front of the house. A door opened on my right, and there stood the younger woman I'd seen at school. Behind her was a huge piano. The image of her face is seared in my mind: a calm expression of perfect resignation, the same look she had on the day of Joey's fight.

Then I heard Mr. Karewski stomping up the steps, bellowing incoherently. As I reached the end of the banister railing, there in a doorway on my left in the dimness was the tiny old woman. She squinted at me and screamed, "Oh God! Oh God! Joe's coming!"

A double door with panels of glass was in front of me, looking out onto the small balcony and over the front porch toward the street. I grabbed the doorknob. It was locked or jammed shut. At that moment, Mr. Karewski was charging toward me, yelling, *"Come here, ya goddamn little hog-grubber, you fuckin' little Jack-a-Dandy!"*

A small straight-back wooden chair stood against the wall. I grabbed the chair by its back and swung it at him. He caught it easily with one hand and turned it to his advantage, throwing his weight into it and pinning me against the balcony's shut doors. I felt the doors giving way behind me, and then I was falling backwards onto the small balcony. He lunged and landed on top of me.

My head was pressed against the balustrades of the balcony's front. The splintered doors were partly on me, and Mr. Karewski was on top of the doors, his arms cut and bleeding from the broken glass of the door's window panes. He snarled and beat at me, trying to pull me up and back into the house. I locked my hands on the balustrades of the balcony. As we struggled, the balcony began groaning and shaking, slowly twisting away from its rotten moorings against the house. And then it began crashing toward the porch's brick floor below.

As the balcony collapsed and fell, it somehow twisted so that I was on top of Mr. Karewski, our limbs entwined, when we hit the porch below. The back of his head smacked against the brick floor like a cantaloupe hurled onto pavement. The sound was not like an apple firmly hitting a stone wall. Nor was it like a squishy tomato splattering into something solid. It was a THWONK like a cantaloupe or even a watermelon bursting. Inches away from me as we lay there, Mr. Karewski's eyes and mouth were open and motionless. He was like a dog hit in the road with everything still in place but, somehow, gone forever.

Stunned for a moment, I did not move but lay listening, waiting for something else to fall. Under me, stinking, Mr. Karewski remained motionless. Rain poured down just beyond the porch, and I could hear the dogs in high bedlam and the piercing screams of the bird. Up above I saw the younger woman of the house standing in the opening where the balcony had been, looking down at us, silently, expressionless.

Then the front door opened. Anna and Maria, wildly surreal in their ballet dresses and with painted faces, stood looking; their mouths were open in fear and confusion. Anna rushed to Mr. Karewski and kneeled beside him without touching him. "Good God!" she screamed, looking back at Maria. "*Good God*!" Then her screams melded with the barking and screeching as she threw herself against the side of the house next to the front door and began beating the wood with her fists. A small, tremulous whimper emerged from her hysteria: "Whata we do?"

But Maria's reaction was different. "Sam, you gotta get outa here," Maria said calmly, speaking over the raging noise of dogs and the bird and the whimpering Anna. If Maria was afraid or upset she did not show it as she stood in the rubble of the collapsed balcony, with me still sprawled across Joe Karewski.

"Is he dead?" I screamed at Maria as I disentangled myself.

"I don't know but I'm telling you to *GO!*" she yelled at me. She grabbed my hand and pulled me off Mr. Karewski and out of the debris. Using the hem of her ballerina dress, she brushed me up and down, pausing quickly to glance at some scrapes and patches of blood on my arms and shirt. "It don't matter if he's dead or alive, you gotta get out of here!"

"Where're the dogs, I hear them!"

"Still chained," she said. "Poppa just *says* he turns them loose. You hurt anywhere?"

"I think I'm okay," I said. For several moments, we both looked down at Mr. Karewski who lay face up on the bricks, his mouth and eyes open, blood seeping from his nose and ears.

"Take your papers and *run!*" Maria said, thrusting the canvas sack toward me, along with my raincoat and the Jim's Diner hat. I suddenly felt overwhelmed, biting my quivering bottom lip, trying to keep at bay the emotions swarming through my whole body.

We stood looking at each other. She was a little taller than I and, to my mind, at least as I look back, the most beautiful girl I'd ever seen—beautiful in the sunshine on the playground and beautiful as she stood here smeared with mascara in the shattered horror of her family. A little older and much wiser than me, Maria was a grownup and I was still a kid.

"*Run!*" she said again, thumping me hard on my chest.

"What about...."

"*Just GO!....*"

"But what are you...."

With this, she clenched the neck of my shirt in her hands and pulled my face to hers: "The only thing I cannot handle is YOU being HERE. Get out of here before the law or the rescue squad comes and forget you ever came here to see the fuckin' dancin' bear!"

With that, Maria's eyes softened briefly and she pressed her mouth hard against mine. Though it lasted only seconds, to me it encompassed all the years she had stoked my confused and private thoughts about her. It mattered not whether it was a motherly kiss or a real girl kiss.

"Now," she said softly, urgently, "Just go!"

I tore off the porch into the rain, running past the snarling dogs straining at their chains. I ran and splashed along the wet streets toward home, the sweet rain doing its best to wash away what was the most horrible experience of my life.

That night at supper, my parents and grandfather were engrossed in a hot debate about a school bond proposal to pay for fixing up our schools. My grandfather explained to me about bonds, but my mind was elsewhere, hoping no one would notice some badly skinned places on my arms and legs. When I had reached our house earlier, before anyone saw me, I called to my mother from the kitchen that I was going to take a hot bath since I was soaked from the rain.

Then at the supper table, Grandfather, as he often did on Thursday evenings after my paper deliveries, used his hackneyed little way of asking if I'd picked up any news in Bog Town, which lay to the west of Shaw's Pond. "All quiet on the western front?" he asked cheerfully.

"Yessir," I said. "All's quiet in Bog Town. Nothin' goin' on but a lot of wet rain."

"He took a hot bath before supper," Mother announced to the table. Turning to my father, she added, "I think it's ridiculous for him to deliver papers in such a rainstorm."

"He's tough," my father said, grinning. "Won't hurt him."

Anna and Maria were not at school the next day, or for the next week. That next night at our supper table the school bond discussion had been displaced by big news from Bog Town. "That sorry old Joe Karewski got killed yesterday," my father reported as soon as he came in.

"What on earth happened?" my mother said.

"He was working on that old house, trying to fix that little balcony over the front porch? And he fell from the second floor. Landed smack on head. Killed him right off."

Grandfather broke the small pause that followed this news. "Peculiar folks, those Karewskis," he said. "Claimed they were circus people, but who knows. I always thought they were gypsies, but I guess they could be both. Showed up around here when I was a boy, and folks said they brought a dancin' bear, but I don't know. Folks'll say anything."

Then his eyes brightened: "But I did like listening to the way old Joe talked. He had an ad and when he'd come in to pay, he always referred to the paper as the Yelper. Tickled me. I guess we do yelp sometimes."

"Too bad if that shoe shop closes," my father said.

"He's got a boy who'll probably run it," Mother said. "Sammy, don't you know the boy?"

"Yessum, name's Joey, but I've just seen him around."

"I shouldn't say this," Mother said. "But, Mister Karewski was not a good man. I had some first-hand dealings, and I can say....."

"Come on, now," Grandfather said. "Let's remember that Mister Karewski had some little children, didn't he? They'll need some help, and we'll need to do something for them."

"Yes, of course," Mother said. "Two Karewski girls are in Sam's school but thank goodness we never let Sam have anything to do with them, isn't that so?" she said, looking at me smugly, as if to remind me of the wisdom of her warnings.

"Yessum," I said. "That's right."

******

Looking back on what happened nearly forty years ago, I remember every smell, every word, and every touch. I can conjure up my abject terror over what this monster, Joe Karewski, threatened to do that rainy afternoon. I can feel Mishka's dry snout and see his toothless grin. I can hear the screams of the bird. I can feel myself on the falling balcony in a violent bear hug with Mr. Karewski. And I can hear the THWONK of the back of his skull on the bricks. Spraddled across him, smothering in his foul stink, thinking he would rise again and kill me, those are things I'll never forget.

41

But Maria's kiss, that peculiar expression of something so undefined, is as sharply pictured in my mind as any of the rest of it.

My role in what happened to Joe Karewski was never revealed, nourishing the common presumption around town that he was working on the rickety balcony when it collapsed. There was no reason for an investigation. The bond of secrecy among those of us present that day was easily kept by a family that had no doubt lived in secret shame for generations. As for me, the gatekeeper for my silence was the soulful despair I felt over what my folks would think about my betrayal of them and the utter stupidity of getting myself into such a situation. I realize it is fair to say that I killed Joe Karewski.

Today, Joey runs the cobbler's shop. Like his father, he comes in each month to pay for his small newspaper ad. Unlike his father, he is subdued, even subservient, in responding to friendliness. He and his wife, a girl from Scuffleton, have two children and live in the old Karewski house along with the pretty woman who is either his mother or his older sister or maybe just someone stolen. They stay to themselves. Joe is buried in the backyard, near the garden, where the old woman I saw that day was put to rest several years after Joe's death.

Little Anna, so frail and sad, left Shaw's Pond many years before I returned. I can't imagine anything good ever happened to her. Had she stayed, I think our town would have made a place for her. Or at least I like to think we would have.

As you know, I run the newspaper and live with my mother in the family house overlooking Shaw's Pond. We get along well, though my mother pines for her two grandchildren who live so far away. And she stews over whether I will ever find a new wife.

Maria lives here in Shaw's Pond with her husband, who works at a factory a few miles away. For years, she has run a small children's daycare business from her house and is well respected in the town and in her church. She has grown into a handsome woman with a well-toned complexion, a little gray in her ebony hair, and a bright smile in her eyes. She dresses nicely and moves gracefully. The odd lilt in her voice reminds me of our long-ago schoolyard days and my enchantment over the little Karewski girls.

I'd like to know more about Maria and how she has managed to survive the horrors I witnessed that day. But when I see her around town, or at the post office, we speak of other things. Surely we both think of that terrible afternoon I learned her family's secrets and fought with her father as he met his gruesome death. But since that afternoon, she and I have never spoken of what happened.

Oddly, I still wonder about Maria's kiss. There was something almost mystical about its extraordinary context. It was much more than a daring, playful schoolyard kiss. It was a real kiss, expressing her feelings I would like to understand. Maybe she meant nothing more than relief and gratitude for the fact an unimaginable burden had just been lifted from her life. After all, I had fought with her evil father and killed him. Or maybe it was nothing more than a way to make me get out of there before some authority arrived and everything suddenly became vastly more complicated.

Each time I see Maria, I wonder whether she even remembers the kiss. Someday I might ask her.

III

Before the Bar

A tobacco farmer from Scuffleton, Dillard Grubb stood slumped before Circuit Court Judge George Washington Shaw. The majesty of the 150-year-old courtroom, decorated with gilded tobacco leaves shining from high molded cornices, was muted by the banality of the ritual at hand. A gaunt figure with gnarled knuckles and unkempt black eyebrows, Dillard Grubb appeared smothered by the stiff gray suit that hung about his spare frame like loose canvas. He had accepted Judge Shaw's offer to let him speak before being sentenced for the ax-murders of his wife, his stepson and a prominent church deacon.

"You tellin' me, Judge, I can say what I been tryin' to say all day, that right?" Grubb's arms hung straight down his sides, and he leaned toward the judge as he spoke. His voice was thin, but calm. Without a hat on his head, a distinct line crossed the top of his forehead, delineating sun baked skin from the sallow white of his upper face.

"Mister Grubb, you may make a statement before the court pronounces its sentence." Judge Shaw busied himself with papers as he spoke. His little blue eyes flicked up once at the man before him. A pair of bailiffs, both major physical presences, kept unctuous eyes upon the prisoner. The spectators who filled the courtroom were silent.

"Well, I got right much to say, 'cause y'all ain't let me tell it straight," said Grubb, his voice growing stronger. "To start with, I'm a peaceable man. Always minded my own business. Never hurt nothin' or nobody. 'Til all this come up. And I tell you one thing, Judge, if them people I killed done to you what they done to me over all these years, you'd a-killed 'em ever one."

Judge Shaw looked up sharply. "Now Mister Grubb, I'm going to let you speak, but keep in mind that you have had your trial and been found guilty. We're not going to have the trial all over again. You took the witness stand and gave your version of events...."

"I was aimin' to tell what happened," Dillard Grubb interrupted, his voice going louder. "But y'all didn't let me explain nothin'. Between you and that other fella over there, that 'ere persecutor, kept bustin' into what I was trying to explain, y'all never let me tell you what it was they done to me."

"The charges were against you, not the victims," Judge Shaw said. "You were charged with murder, two counts of first-degree murder and one of second degree murder." Judge Shaw glanced at the murder weapon lying on the clerk's evidence table and sporting the state's red exhibit tag. The ax blade shimmered with sharpness, and Dalton's eyes followed the judge's who then continued: "You have testified that you committed these heinous crimes, and you have now been convicted by the jury. I'm sure your attorney, Mister Pickeral Chumbley, has made all this clear to you."

"*Pickle Chumbley!*" Dillard Grubb shouted, looking fiercely at his court-appointed lawyer. "Why he's the worst thing that's happened to me since I got here! Judge, you and your crowd are the ones that put Pickle Chumbley on me to start with, and you and everbody here knows he ain't worth a shit!" The big bailiffs ruffled themselves at the profanity, but Judge Shaw ignored it.

Pickeral Chumbley, wearing one of his elegant courtroom suits, rose slightly from his seat to a half-crouch. His fingers sparkled with rings. Bracelets jingled as he moved his hands. His cufflinks were heavy gold chunks—one a replication of a law book, the other the Holy Bible. His tie clasp was in the design of an icon of Blind Justice holding a set of scales that actually bobbed up and down, twinkling under the lights as Pickeral Chumbley moved about.

"Yo' Honah, we done the very best we could under the circumstances, if you know what I mean," Chumbley said with syrupy patience. "But Mister Grubb, now don't get me wrong, yo' Honah, Dillard Grubb is a fine gentleman, and I respect him as my client, but he declined to go along with our defense strategy which would have gone to the question of his mental competence, even his sanity...."

"Obviously, you respect him more than he respects you," offered Judge Shaw, yielding a faint smile. "Let's get on with this, Mister Grubb. You go ahead with your statement, but we're not going to start the trial over."

"Well, I ain't exactly got what y'all call a statement, and I ain't sayin' what happened is *easy* to explain," Grubb said. "But you all still don't know how it all started. It ain't just what happened that day, but all them days and weeks and years that led up to it, all them years they was pickin' at me and stealin' from me. They tricked me into marryin' that woman and then used her to steal my house and farm. That's what you have to know about."

Dillard Grubb's head sank slightly, the canvas-like suit swallowing another inch of his neck. His energy flagged as he looked around the elegant courtroom filled mainly with church friends of Deacon Flournoy Bobbitt, one of the victims. He saw a few friendly neighbors from Scuffleton, including a woman named Dubber Craft who had worked in the Scuffleton store and had always been nice to him.

Then Dillard Grubb raised his eyes to Judge Shaw: "Look like if you was goana gimme a lawyer to help me, you woulda give me somebody that could explain everthing for me." Grubb leaned around and shot a scathing look at Pickeral Chumbley, then turned back to the judge and continued: "All y'all in here talk so easy and pretty. Y'all's talking sounds sweet as songbirds, and y'all can jest talk and talk and talk, and a lot of people come in here don't know what you're talkin' about. Some of us regular folks come in here all worn-out and mad to start with, and we don't know how to talk and explain like y'all do. Askin' me to talk like y'all is like askin' me to fly one of them airplanes."

"Well, Mister Grubb, you'll just have to do the best you can, and I'm getting a little impatient with this. I have a petition for *certiorari* to consider as well as a request for a *capias* order that I want to get to before we break for lunch, so let's move along with your statement."

Dillard Grubb stood staring at the magnificent burled paneling of the judge's bench. His mind wandered to the kind of wood it might be and what might have been done to it to make it shimmer like something soft and alive. "Awright, Judge," Grubb said. "I see it ain't worth gettin' into. It don't matter what I say if I can't say it as pretty as all y'all talk."

He turned wearily and went back to his chair at the defense table and sat down, turning his body away from Pickeral Chumbley. A towering bailiff moved to a spot immediately behind Grubb's chair. Judge Shaw then ordered Dillard Grubb to rise and be sentenced.

Six Months Earlier, Near Scuffleton, Virginia:

Fly circled and collapsed, her sagging teats plastered against the sun-baked clay road. Dillard Grubb looked at the silver-colored pocket watch he was holding and then studied the sun for a moment. "It ain't but four o'clock old time," he said to Fly. "We can rest awhile."

They stayed under the shade tree along the road for about an hour. The old man squatted and kept watch over the parched red earth between his feet. The fly dog stretched out at the edge of the shade patch. Now and then she offered a lazy snap at a slow fly. Dillard Grubb looked up once when the shadow of a cloud caught his eye. He watched the dark cloud travel across the clear sky until it was lost in the leaves of the shade tree. He spoke to Fly and told her the cloud was too high and moving too fast to bring any rain.

Gnats and flies competed for the thick, yellowish milk that seeped from the dog's teats. The insects would have been on the old man if she were not along. It was nearly a month since he had stuffed Fly's seven puppies into a feed sack, tied the top and thrown them off Cobbett's Rock into the Nolting River. He told Fly, who was a long, narrow yellow dog, that he was doing a kindness for both her and the puppies. He told her that so many extra dogs already hung around Scuffleton that seven new ones, all at once like this, would never find their own places. And drowning the pups would save Fly from having to fool with them. On this hot afternoon, only a few of Fly's teats were still dribbling milk, but she still made the old man a good fly dog.

Dillard Grubb thought about the rage his young wife Rachel would be in over his going off all day honey hunting and taking both the fly dog and the watch. Since marrying Grubb and settling in on his farm at Scuffleton eight years earlier, Rachel Grubb had just about destroyed his life. No longer could he peacefully wander the woods searching for lighterwood and honey in the fall, and mushrooms in the spring. Nor could he sit in his own house--a framed-over, two-story log building that became his when his mother finally died--and keep his own quiet company. With Rachel around, along with the boy born a few months after their marriage, peace and quiet had become rank strangers. It was all Grubb could do to pull himself together to scratch out a little tobacco crop to bring in some cash. He and a few other dirt farmers around William Byrd County in Southside Virginia were among the last of those who made small crops and cured the tobacco in wood-fired curing barns.

Agnes Grubb, Dillard's mother, had lingered long in her last illness, and Dillard, her only child, struggled to be dutiful. Neighbors helped, and even the preacher came once a week to sit and pray and, now and then, to find time for a meal. But visitors always seemed to arrive bearing a gloom that settled throughout the house like dust and stayed long after they departed. This gloom also settled over Dillard and quenched whatever lively little sparks that might have ignited his spirits. At one point, early in his mother's illness, Dillard brought her a litter of kittens, thinking their antics might improve her spirits. And they did for a little while. But Agnes seemed to become nervous about this faint joy and asked her son to get rid of the kittens. He did—for their own good as well as his mother's. The Grubbs were practical people.

Alone after Agnes Grubb's death, Dillard got along pretty well. By then he was nearly thirty years old and generally stayed home by himself, venturing out to do a little farming and to go to the store. The only people who came to the house were those who had seen after his mother, and they gradually drifted away. The last time he went to church was for his mother's funeral. As he kept more to himself, he even came to resent being called by his nickname, Dilly, short for Dillard. Some people enjoyed taking the next step and calling him Silly Dilly.

Dillard did not do much reading, though he enjoyed looking at his picture book about dinosaurs, a children's book left at his house once by a group of ladies from Shaw's Pond who were prowling the county combating illiteracy. He had taken an immediate liking to dinosaurs and wondered how people could be so sure none were left. *How can you know when somethin' ain't,* he reasoned, *when there's so many places nobody has looked?* In his wanderings, he was always on the lookout for dinosaurs.

In general, Dillard Grubb felt that people treated him all right. He knew that some considered him curious, even *quaar,* as they called it. Sometimes, when he was at the Scuffleton store, where he liked to sit with a cold drink, some of the men poked a little fun his way. But their comments were not hard or hateful, and he never heard anyone call him Silly Dilly. If they called him that, it was not to his face. In fact, he took their teasing as a sign they sort of liked him.

All in all, the twenty-some years between Agnes Grubb's death and the arrival of Rachel had been uneventful. Dillard's biggest trouble may have been in his head and the way his mind ran from place to place—always thinking about things that didn't make any sense to anyone else. That was one reason he never said much, fearing that people might think something was wrong with him, even that he might be a little "tetched." On the other hand, because so little had ever happened to Dillard, and because he had seen and heard so little, he had a gift for vividly remembering everything he had seen and heard.

In the years just prior to his marriage to Rachel and her arrival at Scuffleton, Dillard had come to admire a girl named Dubber Craft who worked in Clem Witcher's store right there at the Scuffleton crossroads. She had a sweet smile and silky brown hair that had a way of catching any light in the room. Bantering easily, she held forth with grace and energy around the store, and some called her the Belle of Scuffleton.

Dubber always called Dillard Mister Grubb and would sometimes look right at him warmly and ask what he had been up to. Once, he brought her a jar of honey drawn from a fallen tree he had chopped open with his ax. She was gracious and squeezed his hand as she thanked him, leaving him forever enchanted.

Like the dinosaurs, women were among the mysteries Dillard Grubb puzzled over. When he was roaming through the woods, most anything—the shape of a tree, the angle of an old stump--could make him start thinking about women. If he was walking along behind a mule while plowing, he could get to thinking about women. A bull honoring a cow always stirred such thoughts. He puzzled over why he couldn't get his mind off of them. And after all his years of puzzling, he still knew next to nothing about them. He just knew they had something that caused a stirring in his groin and made him want to know more.

Then came the pretty spring afternoon when, while wandering, Dillard came upon the silky-haired Dubber at a secluded tobacco barn in the woods off an abandoned dirt road. She was with a boy he had seen hanging around the store. He had first heard them laughing, and then he saw them wrestling around on the wooden bench under the open tobacco shed and removing some of their clothes. What they did next created a vision in Dillard Grubb's mind that would be with him forever. Secretly, he watched them until they finished what they were doing, got dressed, and walked hand-in-hand up the dirt lane toward where the boy had left his truck. The sight was seared into Grubb's mind so clearly that he could return to it at will, like pulling a treasured photograph from a wallet.

The next day, Dubber, friendly as ever, was working at Clem Witcher's store as if nothing unusual had happened to her. But to old man Grubb, she would never look the same. He took to going to the store more often. Now and then, when the boy came in to chat with her, Grubb stole glances at them to refine certain details in his mental picture.

What Dillard Grubb saw that spring afternoon contributed mightily to the fierce itch that came on him to find a woman to share his bed and, perhaps, to help take care of things around his house. It was an itch, he came to know after meeting Rachel, that he would have been better off finding another way to scratch.

No one around Scuffleton knew where Rachel had started out in life, but they knew that Dillard Grubb had found her eight miles away at Bog Town, a settlement just west of the town of Shaw's Pond, the seat of William Byrd County. She worked at a place called Preacher DeLano Hairston's Lunch, more commonly known as "The Lunch," or even "De Lunch," which usually, when spoken, came out as *D'Lunch*. Grubb's cousin, Willie Dawson, who treated himself to monthly visits to D'Lunch, recommended the place, saying he thought it would settle Dillard's nerves if he paid a visit now and then. Willie Dawson offered to take Dillard and make an introduction, since, as a protection against police raids, the place operated on personal referrals.

The first time they visited D'Lunch, the cousins drove to Bog Town on Willie Dawson's truck. As a regular patron, Dawson arrived knowing which girl he would favor, and Preacher DeLano Hairston consented to his request right away and rounded her up. But before the bashful Dillard could voice his pick of one of the three remaining women who sat before him, Preacher Hairston told him he was in for a special treat reserved for first-timers. He told Dillard that D'Lunch's ever-popular Sally-Do had spotted him when he came in, spoken for his company, and was awaiting him in one of the rear rooms.

The encounter turned out to be a little different from what Dillard Grubb had in mind. Sally-Do was a short, heavily built black woman with gray-streaked hair, blue gums and no teeth. Though Grubb had little choice in what transpired, he did tell himself that perhaps this was as good a way as any to get started fooling with women. On the way home, Willie Dawson explained that what Dillard had gotten from Sally-Do was a regular feature at D'Lunch. It was called the Blue Gum Special.

It was on that visit to D'Lunch that Grubb first saw Rachel. She was not considered particularly pretty, though Preacher Hairston, the owner of the house, bragged shamelessly about certain of her other attributes. Rachel had a thin face, dark close-set eyes, a tight mouth and prominent ears set at nearly right angles to the sides of her head. She usually spoke in quick bursts, creating an impression of snapping at the person she was speaking to.

Cousin Willie Dawson strongly warned Dillard to stay away from her. He said the word around was that Rachel was pregnant by Preacher Hairston and that the holy man was looking to "get her gone" any way he could. She was said to be high-tempered and to have caused trouble around the place, fighting and squabbling with customers as well as staff. Dawson warned Dillard that if Rachel or Preacher Hairston found out that he was the owner of a house and farm at Scuffleton, his property as well as the rest of his life could be in jeopardy.

A few weeks after his initial visit, Dillard Grubb went back to D'Lunch by himself, making the trip on his tractor. Rachel, evidently having been tipped off that Dillard was an unusually eligible bachelor, was lying in wait for him. On that day, Preacher Hairston greeted Dillard and introduced him to a smiling, engaging Rachel, cleaned up and on her best behavior.

Preacher Hairston smiled and patted Dillard on the shoulder and whispered quietly, "Now this is a gal who can put some real snap in your noodle!"

Rachel told him she had seen him on his earlier visit, admired him, and had wanted to get to know him. She led Grubb to her room, sat him down on the edge of her bed and explained that she had a special liking for men like him. Eager, ready with his money, Dillard was completely surprised when Rachel declined it. She said that when she first laid eyes on him during his last visit, a feeling of infatuation came over her more intense than she had ever experienced. She told Dillard she would never have relations with a man she really cared for unless they were married.

But that did not stop Rachel from a frenzy of hugging and kissing with her new love as they sat there on the edge of the bed. When she stuck her tongue in Dillard's mouth, he spat it out, complaining that it felt like a fish was sucking on his tongue. Rachel told Dillard she was so steamed up that she could hardly control herself. As for Dillard, he was in such a hot frazzle that he found himself wondering if old Sally-Do might be available that afternoon. In the end, Rachel explained that given the heat of their feelings for each other, along with her personal standards, marriage was the only proper way to go forward.

Pixilated, Dillard Grubb mounted his tractor and headed back to Scuffleton. He thought about the friendly warning from Willie Dawson to stay away from Rachel, but that was weak music compared to the fact that, for the first time in his life, Dillard was in love.

A few days later, a rare smile lighted his sad face when he went to Clem Witcher's store to use the telephone. Dubber was behind the counter. He asked her to place a call to Preacher Hairston at D'Lunch and to hand him the phone. He instructed her to put the long-distance call on his account.

Dillard could sense a caution in Dubber's demeanor. He glanced up and saw that she was looking at him in that warm, friendly way of hers. "Now Mister Grubb," she said. "I don't know what you fixin' to do, but somethin' tells me that old big possum might walk tonight, and we wouldn't want nothin' to happen to you." Her eyes and smile showed a concern that gave Dillard a small pause, even a little shiver of uncertainty. "That old Preacher Hairston and that whore-house of his has got a lot of good people in trouble," Dubber said. "You know that, now don't you?"

Dillard's face sagged and his mouth twitched. His vision of Dubber and her boyfriend intruded for an instant. And he thought of how his long-dead father used to speak ominously of nights when the big possum might walk. It was not a good sign, but Dillard was too far along to change his course. After Dubber placed the call and handed him the phone, he held it down in the top of his overall bib and mumbled into it until Dubber politely moved to the other end of the counter.

Several days later, as arranged, Dillard Grubb traveled to Bog Town to get his bride. His cousin, Willie Dawson, drove him and let him off at D'Lunch but did not wait. Ever gracious, Preacher Hairston greeted Dillard and offered to drive the couple to the courthouse at nearby Shaw's Pond in his new Oldsmobile. At the clerk's office, Preacher Hairston did all the necessary talking and then served as the witness to the marriage. By this time, Rachel appeared to be about six months along in her rumored pregnancy.

"There's just one more thing," Preacher Hairston said to the newlyweds. "While we're here in the clerk's office, I've had some papers drawn up for y'all to sign. Just regular business when folks fall in love and get married."

Dillard Grubb felt a sure confidence in Preacher Hairston, a tall, tan-colored Negro man with thin lips, grayish eyes and long, graceful hands and fingers. His movements were fluid as he whipped out some papers. A flick of his eyebrows brought a clerk over to the counter who, the preacher said, would make everything official. All the transaction would do, he explained to the couple, was to make the newlyweds joint owners of each other's property.

"Completely routine," Preacher Hairston said, smiling, as he handed Dillard Grubb a stout gold pen with which to sign his name. It was a high moment for Dillard, standing in the William Byrd County Courthouse with his new bride, signing important papers with a gold pen. Dillard tried for a moment to roll the pen through his fingers gracefully as he had seen Preacher Hairston do, but his fingers were too stubby and crooked. It wasn't clear to Dillard what property Rachel brought to the union, but the transaction did include his own house and farm.

They all hurried back to D'Lunch, where old Sally-Do greeted them. She had gotten Rachel's belongings together in several sacks and an old suitcase. Preacher Hairston said he would like to drive the newlyweds home to Scuffleton if they could leave right away, since, the preacher said, he was short on time and had an important appointment elsewhere.

Bearing the vanity plate "DE LUNCH," Preacher Hairston's dark Oldsmobile glided smoothly over the eight miles to Scuffleton. "Now, y'all understand, I cain't go down no dirt roads to a house," the preacher explained. "I just got a wash job, so I'll let y'all off at the road."

"Yessir," said Dillard from the back seat. He thought it might be the first time he had ever said "sir" to a Negro. "Just let us off at Clem Witcher's Store," Dillard said, "I have a lot of friends there and we might can find somebody to take us the rest of the way."

With a flourish, Preacher Hairston pulled into the old wood-frame store where men--chewing, talking and spitting--sat in little clutches along the wide front porch. But that all ceased as the men's eyes fixed upon the unfolding spectacle before them. After Dillard Grubb emerged from the back seat, Rachel emerged from the other back door--big-bellied and already looking angry.

"Looky yonder," Dubber said to Clem Witcher as the newlyweds stood beside Rachel's belongings piled in front of the store. She pointed toward the scene unfolding just outside the store's front window. "I told old Silly Dilly the big possum was fixin' to walk, and just look at them two standin' there. That big possum, he done walked for sure, and somebody's goana get walked all over before this is done with."

Now, on this day, eight years later, Dillard Grubb squatted there in the road with his fly dog and listened to Rachel yelling for them from down at the house about a quarter-mile away. He couldn't be sure what she was saying, but he figured she was threatening to refuse him his supper if he didn't get home right then.

He looked at the watch, told Fly the time, and they started along a path through the woods to the house. Grubb's felt hat, with cooling holes punched in the sides, was jerked down tightly over his brow. He carried an ax loosely at his side, and the head of it struck rotten stumps as they shuffled through the woods. Fly's bony haunches pistoned up and down as she loafed along in front of Grubb with her nose to the ground. When they neared the hog pen, two of the lean animals grunted to the edge of the wallow and pushed against the fence, their little eyes ever hopeful.

Just as they passed the hen house and went into the clearing, Rachel barged off the stoop and rushed toward them, meeting them right at the well. "You goanna tell me you been off honey huntin' all day, and you goanna tell me that dog followed you and you couldn't help it, and how you had to take the watch with you, well I ain't hearin' none of it, and you sure ain't gettin' nothin' to eat around here tonight!"

She strode toward him, one hand clenched at her side, the other pointing at his face: "*Gimme that watch!*" she screeched. Just as she snatched it away, he realized he had not turned the hands forward one hour since that morning when he took it from the kitchen table and set it back on old time. What the radio and TeeVee called Daylight Savings Time was something that puzzled and intrigued him.. *How could anyone change what time it was?* So he set the watch one way, his wife the other. After awhile, neither knew what time it was, not that it mattered much anyway.

Rachel studied the watch face and then looked at the setting sun. "Dillard Grubb," she said, turning toward him, her voice lowering. "I told you what I'd do if you set this watch back again. Just because you an old fashion damn fool don't mean I am. And just 'cause I let you sleep in the house last night, that don't mean you can leave here in the mornin' and take the watch and that fly dog. You know you don't need that dog, and what you think me and the boy can do around here all day if we ain't got the fly dog, *or the watch!*"

Just then, her fat little boy, Frankie, whose shrouded conception had led to Grubb's present circumstances, appeared beside his mother. He was a rather dark-skinned child, carrying far too much weight—even in his hands and cheeks. "I wanna go to the store!" he demanded. "I ain't got nothin' to eat and I'm hungry! *Momma*, make Dilly carry me to the store on the tractor!" The boy glowered at Grubb.

"*Shut up!*" his mother said. "I'm tryin' to talk to this fool went off with our watch all day." Dillard did not like this boy. He had struck him once, about a year ago, and in retaliation Rachel beat her husband with a heavy-duty broken fan belt from the tractor while the boy stood by laughing. "We fixin' to eat right now, but this old fool ain't eatin' with us," Rebecca said. "And he ain't stayin' in the house tonight. He can stay in the woods or up under the house or in the hen house or the smokehouse. I don't care. He just ain't comin' in my house, doin' the way he do!"

"It ain't your house," Grubb said. "It's my house. Momma give it to me. One of these days I'm goanna do somethin' about how you and that Preacher Hairston cooked all this up and stole everthing I got, everthing my folks give me."

"Shut up your fool mouth!" Rachel said. "You ain't goanna do nothin'. *Come on!*" she hollered at the boy. "Let's go eat."

As Rachel turned to leave, she tripped over Fly who was lying behind her. Hopping away on one foot, she hollered, "Goddamn you, Dog. Ain't you got a lick of sense? You a bigger fool than Dillard Grubb!" Rachel got her balance back and yelled again at the dog and told her to come with her. Fly followed her to the house and into the kitchen and worked her way under the table. It was hotter in the kitchen than outside, and soon she was asleep. And the flies flocked to the dog's sticky milk.

The old man was plenty hungry, so while there was still light, he headed by foot over to the tobacco field where he had seen a wild blackberry patch.

He got back to his house about an hour later and recognized Deacon Flournoy Bobbitt's truck in the road by the house. Fly was asleep in the yard. The Deacon didn't like the fly dog—said he didn't believe in fly dogs—and always made Rachel turn Fly out when he came. Nor did the deacon like old man Grubb, finding in him a convenient example of the devil's handiwork. Such targeted evils were in the tradition of the Clustered Congregation Independent Church, where, rather than celebrating the good or even pretending forgiveness, the minister and deacons taught goodness and mercy by damning evil. Deacon Bobbitt was never more sure of himself than when he had Dillard Grubb in his sights.

Grubb knew better than to approach the door to the house and risk an encounter with the deacon. So he headed straight for the crawlspace under the house where he was relegated when Rachel was particularly angry with him, as she was now. If he were not in trouble with her, she would usually let him sleep on the couch by the radio in the front room, but not at times like this.

Fly saw the old man crossing the yard and followed him under the house and stretched out while he spread out the old quilt he kept there for nights like this. The dirt was softer and more comfortable than the hard earth of the yard and road, and he could quickly work his boney body into a comfortable position. In the late evening, as now, stray hens clucked about looking for doodlebugs in the soft dirt before going to roost in the hen house. Grubb shooed them away, and their flutter settled on the opposite side, where the lighterwood and kindling were piled to keep dry.

Grubb could hear voices in the kitchen just above his head—Deacon Bobbitt, Rachel and her son Frankie. He could hear what they were saying about him, the boy reporting that the old man had been off honey hunting again and had taken the watch when he had no use for it. The boy stated that it was a waste of time for the old man, who, he reminded the deacon, was not his real father, to be wandering around in the woods all day. Frankie never passed up a chance to tell that his real father was Preacher Hairston, the prominent businessman and owner of DeLunch in Bog Town.

Deacon Bobbitt was mostly silent, grunting now and then, and Grubb could hear an eating utensil clicking against a plate. He knew that Deacon Bobbitt was filling his big belly with food that might have been Grubb's. When the clicking stopped, Grubb heard the deacon's chair scrape back. The man coughed and hawked and then Dillard heard the drone of his high-pitched voice, one that moved to a keen little yelp when he sought to make a special point.

"Well, I can tell you this Sister Rachel, and this is God's truth. Most sinners can be cured, and the Lord has laid powers on me to do that curin', but you know somethin'? Ain't nothin' nobody can do about the sorriest of the sorry, for the Devil *hisself* is in 'em! I cured a lot of souls in my time, and I can tell you that Dillard Grubb's soul just ain't curable. He's the sorriest of the sorry. I doubt if God *Hisself* could cure such a soul."

One of the hens clucked closer to Dillard, and the old man's jumpy mind went to the pictures of the dinosaurs in his book. Way back when he was a wandering boy, he had discovered the skeleton of a chicken and was mesmerized over how much it looked like the skeleton of the dinosaur in his book. The book even said that dinosaurs laid eggs. Dillard still wondered about it, even now as he watched the hen maneuvering adroitly on her two legs. He had learned to keep such wonderings to himself, and shooed the hen away.

With the voices droning above him, Dillard thought about the years when his mother and father were alive and they all sat at that same joyless table. His father was a good farmer, his mother read the Bible, and they made their only child go to school until he quit, telling them he had learned enough. But there was never any music, or joy, and hardly ever a smile. At church, they sat on the back row and left quickly without lingering and talking. Dillard never understood why they were so sad, so different, but he knew that they were.

He dozed off to the tune of the listless chatter above him, and by and by, he awakened to hear chairs scraping on the floor. Deacon Bobbitt announced that it was ten-thirty. Rachel sent the boy upstairs to bed. Lying on his back, the old man could see specks of light winking through from the rough pine floor above, coming from worn places in the linoleum that he had been supposed to fix to stop the cold air in the winter.

As the deacon left, Rachel followed him out onto the front porch. In lowered tones of reverence, the deacon said, "Tell me, Sister, can you feel God's presence? I feel His power, the power of the Holy Ghost, right here with us, and it's been more'n a month since we worked on cleanin' and curin' your own soul, Sister, and I think we oughta do it tonight."

"That'd be awright with me," Rachel said, "long as you bring a rubber. And don't come back here 'til late, 'cause that boy ain't been sleepin' in all this heat and I want him to be asleep."

"Don't you worry," the deacon said. "The Lord'll watch over us and keep us, and now I'm goanna ride over and check my barn. I got a curin' of tobacco to watch over, but I'll be back."

By then, they had reached the yard and Grubb could not hear what else they were saying. He peered out from under the porch and saw by the light of the rising moon the deacon consulting his handsome gold pocket watch, the kind with the snap-open cover. It was a far fancier watch than the one he had. With a flick of his wrist, a move much like a toss of dice, the deacon snapped the watch shut and became jovial: "It's been nice as rice seein' you and that fine boy of yours, Sister Rachel, and may the Lord watch over you and keep you 'til tonight."

Grubb watched and listened as the truck clattered out the road toward the hard surface. He could hear the tailgate banging as the truck hit ruts in the road, and then he heard the truck stop. It had happened before, and the old man knew he was about to lose some of his hens. Once, after the deacon had visited his wife, Grubb was sitting up at the hen house and saw the deacon stuff two squawking hens into a burlap bag. Usually, the deacon would come back a day or so later and present Rachel with a freshly killed hen in the name of Lord, and she would pluck it and cook it for him. But since the old man and the fly dog had to leave the house whenever the deacon came, Grubb never got even a taste of the cooked chicken.

The squawking the old man now heard from the hen house subsided as the truck cranked up and clattered off. Fly had gotten up and stood there with Grubb looking in the direction of the hen house. "That's awright girl," he told her. "He don't usually take but two. But I'm powerful tired of the way these folks do me, and been doin' me for a long time."

Old man Grubb's hunger was heavy now, and he had heard what the deacon said about going to his curing barn. Grubb figured there would be some roasting ears in the coals of the barn's firebox, and he knew the deacon would be leaving to come back to see Rachel. Grubb figured a roasting ear would be just right. He laced up his boots and got his ax. Fly followed him out of the yard and up the long hill to the road. The moon was just getting up.

When they got to the deacon's barn nearly an hour later, Deacon Bobbitt was sitting on the bench facing the two open fires of the curing barn. The air was thick with stinging wood smoke and the moist aroma of curing tobacco. Grubb saw the deacon aimlessly whittling on a piece of wood, occasionally puckering his lips and spewing a stream of tobacco spit toward the fire.

A jar of whiskey sat on the bench beside him. The top was off. This was the first time Grubb had ever seen the deacon without his hat, and the long, thick gray-black hair was sweat-matted along his temples. His ruddy complexion was flushed by the heat and the whiskey.

After a bit, when Deacon Bobbitt got up to tend the fire, the old man's heart quickened when he spotted a clutch of roasting ears in the coals of one of the fireboxes. They were getting just about right, he thought, since the first few layers of the crisp shucks had peeled. But, oddly, in the presence of such a scoundrel, Grubb's hunger had diminished, or at least was different. In its place was a mental keenness, a fresh feeling of something akin to confidence.

Peering through its branches and leaves, Grubb squatted under a leafy green dogwood tree across the dirt lane from the barn, Fly was snoozing beside him. When the deacon finished stoking the fire, he turned and walked straight for the old man and the dog. He unbuttoned his overalls as he crossed the lane. Grubb knew what the deacon was going to do, but he realized that if he moved he would be found out. So he continued squatting and rested a hand on Fly, hoping he could keep her from moving.

Then it started, splattering against the smooth leaves and on the old man's hat, and then the leaves gave in and the stinking stream of urine hit squarely on one of his knees. Fly had not moved, but when the stream hit her directly, she scrambled into the open and cowered, looking up at the deacon. The deacon jumped back at first, and then he recognized the dog.

"Get away from me!" he shouted, his voice going to a high yelp. Fly scuttled back into the hiding place, and that's when the deacon saw the old man squatting there. "Well, God bless my soul!" he screeched. "Looky here, old Silly Dilly, come on outa there. If I'd a known you was in there, I'd come over here and pissed on you sooner!" Deacon Bobbitt laughed as he waggled his member at Grubb, as if to threaten a new dousing.

Anger flashed through Grubb, but he was befuddled and at a loss as to how to respond. "You ain't got much of a pecker," Grubb blurted out. "Preachers is supposed to have good-size peckers, but I reckon you just a deacon, not a preacher." Deacon Bobbitt seemed stunned."

"*What you doin' talkin' like that to me, you sorry sonofabitch!*" The deacon advanced and slammed his boot into Grubb's face. The old man fell back on the ground. "You ain't comin' 'round here talkin' about my pecker! You ain't never even fucked your wife. All you fuck is pigs and chickens and knot-holes in trees, probably fuckin' that sorry damn dog!" Deacon Bobbitt ordered his clothes. Rooster-like, he strutted across the lane and washed away his indignation with a hard swallow of whiskey. Bleeding now from his nose, Grubb got himself up and stood in the lane. He left the ax under the dogwood.

"Whatch you doing here?" the deacon said. "Your old lady must of run you off, else wouldn't feed you. What? Was you aimin' on stealin' something of mine to eat? Well, I got some roastin' ears over yonder in the fire, but you ain't getting' none. The Lord deals with people like you and He ain't goanna catch me feedin' the evilness of the devil. He do tell us to feed the stranger and clothe him and wash his feet, because it might be Him come again. But He don't say nothin' about helpin' sorry trash like you!"

Dillard Grubb stood there in the road, Fly cowering behind him. The deacon waved his arms as he preached, and Grubb could smell the foul whiskey on him. When the churchman wiped his brow, he left a white, sweaty streak against his dirty forehead.

"I come after them hens you stole," Grubb said, trying to look the deacon straight in the eye.

The deacon stared back incredulously. He reached for a swallow of whiskey and opened his mouth wide and spread his lips over the rim of the jar and sort of poured the whiskey into the opening. The deacon took the jar away and held it at arm's length and after a few seconds he squenched his face up and swallowed hard, seeming to squirt the liquid down his throat. Then he gritted his teeth and shook his head and coughed. He carefully placed the jar on the bench and turned ceremoniously toward the old man.

"Listen here to me," he said. "That's as low a thing as anybody ever accused me of. Stealin' chickens. I been accused of a lot of things, but I ain't never been accused of stealin' chickens. Whoever heard of a *deacon* stealin' chickens?" Deacon Bobbitt's voice was rising now, his florid face seeming to puff up, even across the forehead. Grubb looked down at the dirt; the back of his left hand was covered with blood from wiping his nose. Fly, attentive, sat at a distance.

"The Lord don't talk to me like He do you," Grubb said. "But I still know you stole my hens. Ain't the first time you done it. And you cain't tell me no different. I come to get them hens you stole tonight." He wiped blood from his nose again.

"You better listen to me real close," Deacon Bobbitt said. "If I had took your chickens, if I *had*, I would of been in the right 'cause I'd of been givin' them to the poor people, the needy people, the shut-in cases that ain't got nothin' to eat. In His own great book, the Lord tells us it ain't nothin' wrong with takin' from the rich and givin' to the poor, so long as the rich is too sorry to give it away themselves. And the Lord, he makes certain ones on this earth to look out for His word, to do His duty, and that's what deacons does."

The old man wiped his nose and shifted his feet but dropped his eyes from the deacon's face. Fly lay watching.

"Let me tell you something, old Silly Dilly. You don't have no idea how important a deacon is. While the preacher gets up and preaches ever Sunday mornin' and Wednesday night, the deacon, he's out amongst the flock, healin' wounds, feedin' hungry mouths, settlin' little differences here and there, and curin' lost souls. And if a deacon comes on a fat hen, and he knows it belongs to a family of plenty and knows of somebody else that ain't got nothin', he owes it to the Lord to pluck that fat hen from the rich and give it to the poor.

"And the Lord tells us about people like you what don't never do nothin'. You go off ever mornin' with that sorry dog and stay gone all day and then you come home at night lookin' for somethin' to eat. The Lord tells us that you supposed to keep your wife well flourished, and I know you ain't never even tried. She told me herself you won't no good."

With that, the deacon lurched toward Fly and slammed his boot into her muzzle. She cried out and slunk closer to Grubb. Relishing the dog's cowering, he moved in and kicked her again and hollered, *"That's from the Lord to your goddamn sorry dog."* Then he went over and took another swallow of whiskey, leaving the dog whimpering against the old man's legs.

Then he paused to stuff a chunk of tobacco into his mouth as he kept an eye on the old man. His jaw and neck muscles strained as he softened the hard plug of tobacco.

The front of Grubb's overalls was still wet from where the deacon urinated on him. He reached up and pulled his damp hat down tighter over his forehead. He studied the grass sprigs in the middle of the dirt lane and murmured, "I still come after them hens."

Deacon Bobbitt went over and stoked the firebox and took another drink from the jar. When he came back, he stepped up close to the old man, cocked himself back and renewed his verbal attack. Only this time Grubb felt a large, wet chunk of tobacco hit his face, just below the eye, and he winced as the deacon laughed furiously.

A pine log snapped in the fire. Grubb's eyes blinked in the stinging smoke, and he shifted his feet and looked up: "All I come here for was to get them hens you took, and now you done busted my nose and kicked my dog. I ain't never done nothin' to you. Somebody'd think you was either drunk or crazy."

Deacon Bobbitt shrieked with laughter and screamed into Grubb's face: "Yeah, and some people might think the Lord could *cure you*, but I know better! Ain't no *curing* things like you! I can tell you right now, Dillard Grubb, the good Lord Jesus Christ is goana see that you burn in hell 'cause he sure ain't got no mansion in heaven for you and your kind!"

Grubb now stared at the deacon. His brows were clinched tight, and his eyes were bloodshot from the harsh wood smoke. His black, bushy eyebrows were prominent against his pale forehead. "I ain't never done nothin' against you or your people," he told Deacon Bobbitt. "I ain't done nothin' against your church, and I ain't done nothin' against the Lord. All I come here for was to get them hens you stole."

With that, old man Grubb wiped at his face again and then headed down the dark lane. Fly followed. Deacon Bobbitt's laughter carried through the night.

When they had almost reached the tar road, the old man and Fly cut across a freshly mown hayfield, and when they got to the woods they kept moving until they came to the big boulder called Cobbett's Rock that hung out over a bend in the Nolting River. Grubb squatted on the rounded, moss-splotched rock and looked down at the water below. The moon had gotten higher and smaller, and its reflection rippled in the water below.

He tried to think about what he always tried to think about lately. How things had gotten so bad and how much longer he could endure it. He had been a man with property--a house and farm of his own and lost it to a woman who had never once been intimate with him. He had never hurt anyone, and his only sin was hanging around the old barn where Dubber liked to meet her boyfriend. But all he'd done was watch them and wish he could find similar pleasure.

In the distance, he heard a truck whining along the tar road and knew it was the deacon on his way to spend some time with Rachel.

A thought from the past came to him. Nobody would care if he just jumped off Cobbett's Rock into the river below and drowned himself, easy, just like when he drowned Fly's puppies. But if by chance the deacon had it right about hellfire and damnation, he figured life like this was better than going to hell any sooner than he had to. He stared at the moon's reflection in the river as it got smaller and smaller, rippling faster and faster. After a while, he heard the deacon's truck out on the tar road, speeding back to the curing barn.

He stood up and looked at the moon. It was high and little, like it had gone cold and blue with almost no light surrounded by heaven's peaceful gallery of twinkling lights. Suddenly, something Dubber had said long ago jumped into his mind, like it had come shooting down from out of the sky. *Will the big possum walk tonight?* He wondered for bit about what that meant.

"Come on," he said to Fly. "Let's go back to the barn. I left my ax layin' up yonder under that dogwood."

They left Cobbett's Rock, the old man, his hunger long gone, moving straight along, Fly ranging a little ahead of him. They crossed the field to the clay road and walked faster until until they reached the last curve before the barn. When they got to the creek, just down the hill from the barn, they stopped, and the old man listened. A single whine from Fly broke the silence, and he quieted her by resting a hand on her head. They started up the hill through the woods and stopped when they got to the dogwood.

Deacon Bobbitt was slouched on the bench, leaning against a post, his head tilted back and his mouth hanging open. His drunken snore sounded like erratic grunts from a hog. The fireboxes were almost dead, and the glow silhouetted the deacon's head. The stinging odor of wood smoke had subsided, leaving the sweet settled smell of cured tobacco.

Grubb picked up his ax and crossed the lane until he was just behind the deacon's head. Holding the ax with both hands over his head, he slowly lowered the sharp edge down to just an inch above the head's balding crown. When he raised the ax again, thoughts flooded his mind about the Lord God Jesus Christ and the Bible and the fly dog and the hens and how Rachel had brought that half-breed boy into his life and stolen his farm. And how she sometimes called him Silly Dilly. Then he slammed the ax down with all his might. The blade slashed into the deacon's skull down to the nose. Blood erupted, and he pulled back and drove the ax down again. He moved around to the front and slammed the ax down until the deacon's upper body seemed split into two pieces.

Then he stopped and looked at the vermilion mass twitching, bubbling like some cauldron of wickedness. Grubb then drove the ax into each half until the legs and arms were nearly severed, and each time he perceived a twitch, he went on chopping until something caught his eye, an object reflecting light from the dying embers of the fire.

The deacon's gold watch had been knocked aside and was lying on top of the stone firebox. Grubb picked it up and flicked open the cover the way he had seen the deacon do. He studied the face of the watch, and it said three o'clock. He knew it was bound to be new time. He turned the hands until they read two o'clock, old time, smiled and snapped the cover shut.

Then he opened it and snapped it shut again. He flicked it open and shut it once more. It was a pretty watch, and it felt good in his hand. His mind jumped to his wedding day and he thought of the stout gold pen and how handsome it was in the graceful fingers of Preacher Hairston. He stepped from the shed and looked at the shining gold cover as it reflected the high moon. He thought about the dinosaurs. The vision of the silky-haired Dubber and her man flicked through his mind. He turned back and pitched the watch into the spreading mass of blood and meat. Then he took a long piss right into the middle of it.

When he finished, Dillard turned and looked at the firebox. With a tobacco stick, he poked around in the coals for a roasting ear. Most had burned to ashes, but he found a piece of an ear. Then he took the jar of whiskey and helped himself to a long drink before tossing what was left onto the embers. A purplish blue flame erupted for a moment and then was gone. He picked up his ax.

"Come on," he said to Fly. "Let's go home."

TRIPLE AX-MURDERER SHOT DEAD IN COURT

By HEZZIE PIGG
William Byrd Tribune Reporter

Like a scene in a wild-west movie, shooting broke out in the William Byrd County Courthouse at Shaw's Pond on Thursday morning. When the smoke cleared, a just-sentenced triple ax-murderer lay dead on the courtroom floor from a volley of bullets fired by Chief Bailiff William Alexander.

Dillard Grubb, a 60-year-old farmer from Scuffleton, had been sentenced to life in prison without parole for the brutal ax-slayings of his wife, stepson and Deacon Flournoy Bobbitt, a close family friend.

In passing the sentence moments before the violence erupted, Judge George Washington Shaw V noted that the convicted triple-murderer had shown "not the slightest remorse or explanation for butchering three human beings, including an innocent eight-year-old boy."

At the very moment Judge Shaw spoke those words, the prisoner Grubb, who had been ordered to stand for sentencing, lunged toward the clerk's evidence table where lay the ax he had used as a murder weapon. Just as he got his hands on the ax and was raising it, Chief Bailiff Alexander fired, hitting Grubb at least twice in the chest. Grubb fell immediately, tumbling forward with the ax still in his hands.

Screams filled the courtroom. Judge Shaw, who had instantly thrown himself beneath the bench when the trouble started, popped up and ordered the courtroom cleared and the rescue squad summoned.

Grubb, who took the stand during his trial, never denied the basic facts of the case or that he was the killer.

In a bloody rampage during the early morning of August 22nd of last year, Grubb first killed Deacon Flournoy P. Bobbitt, 48, a tobacco farmer and prominent Christian leader of the Cobbett's Rock community. Grubb was convicted of attacking Bobbitt as he dozed at a barn where he was watching a curing of tobacco. Dr. H. H. Hammer, the county medical examiner, testified that Mr. Bobbitt's body was so thoroughly disemboweled that it was impossible to determine how many ax strokes had been delivered. "He was chopped all to pieces," Dr. Hammer testified.

Following the murder of Deacon Bobbitt, Grubb traveled by foot several miles across country to the house he shared with his wife, Rachel, 28, and 8-year-old stepson, Frankie Hairston. After axing his wife to death as she slept in her bed, he apparently subdued the boy in the kitchen and killed him there.

Commonwealth's Attorney Posie J. Hundley placed the murder weapon into evidence, as well as numerous photographs of the crime scenes taken by the William Byrd County Sheriff's Office. When the shooting in the courtroom started, Mr. Hundley seemed traumatized and did not move from his seat at the prosecutor's table.

At the defense table, Attorney Pickeral ("Pick") Chumbley, Grubb's court-appointed lawyer, leapt over several rows of seats getting out of the courtroom. "I thought he might be after me with that ax," Mr. Chumbley later stated. Mr. Chumbley had been severely criticized by his client in open court.

Mr. Chumbley said that Grubb, who insisted upon taking the stand to explain why he believed his actions were justified, scuttled his lawyer's plans for a psychiatric defense. Court observers generally agreed that Grubb's testimony, frequently interrupted by Mr. Hundley, the prosecutor, was not coherent.

Observers agree that this likely is the region's first triple-ax murder conviction, though there have been several double ax-murders.

Grubb's wife Rachel, one of the victims, was described as a native of Schoolfield who had worked at Preacher DeLano Hairston's Lunch at Bog Town prior to her marriage eight years ago. She was a homemaker at the time of her death. Her son Frankie Hairston, also murdered, would have been in the second grade.

"Rachel was a fine wife and mother," said Flossie Fletcher of Scuffleton, who attended the trial. "She sort of stayed to herself, but she never caused any trouble. And that little boy was so cute and sweet.

Just a precious child. Sometimes you'd see him ridin' on the back of the tractor with old Dillard, he'd be goin' to the store to get hisself a little piece of candy."

Flournoy Bobbitt, described by the prosecutor as a High Deacon in the Clustered Congregation Independent Holiness Church of Cobbett's Rock, is survived by his wife Iris and four children.

"Flournoy never met a stranger," Mrs. Bobbitt said during a break in the trial. "He loved his fellow man and was never happier than when he was out among the people and goin' about the Lord's work." Mrs. Bobbitt wept throughout the trial.

Deacon Bobbitt's minister, the Holy Reverend Isaac Musick, said he spoke for the entire congregation in his certainty that the killer Dillard Grubb "will be made to endure the horror of the Lord's eternal damnation." Mr. Musick explained that his church does not embrace the concept of redemption for heinous crimes such as this, adding: "This is a case where we witnessed the sinner moments before his earthly death and at the very moment of his death. As this vile sinner breathed his final breath, we can rest in the sure knowledge that his soul was aboard that express train to hell."

Several trial spectators said they would have testified about the peaceful nature of Dillard Grubb, but, they said, his attorney told them his client did not want any character witnesses. One of Dillard Grubb's supporters is Dubber Craft, a storekeeper at Scuffleton, who said she had known Mr. Grubb most of her life and would trust him completely.

"Mr. Grubb was just different," she said later. "He was quiet and humble, but he was a nice, gentle old man who minded his own business. I remember once he brought me a little jar of honey he had taken from a tree trunk, probably with that old ax he always carried around, probably the same ax they had in the courtroom, the one he done it with. I just think there was a lot goin' on with those people, a lot that never came out in the trial. Those people, and I knew all of 'em, every one, picked at Mister Grubb all the time, and they just finally picked too much."

Another trial spectator, the Reverend DeLano Hairston, owner of Preacher Hairston's Lunch at Bog Town, said he was well acquainted with all of the victims and had actually introduced Mr. Grubb to his deceased wife, Rachel, when she was employed at his restaurant. "She was a fine young lady, and we were all happy for her when she met Mr. Grubb and they married and moved to Scuffleton," Mr. Hairston said.

"But we must all pray for Dillard Grubb," Mr. Hairston added. "We must pray for his soul to somehow find Jesus and to be delivered in to heaven on the Chariot of God. Who among us mortals can presume to understand what has happened here, but you can be sure the Lord understands it and has a purpose."

Asked whether he had a connection to Mrs. Grubb's son, Frankie Hairston, Mr. Hairston stated, "I do have a financial interest in the Dillard home house and farm, and I will be taking steps to be sure everything is in order on the worldly end of things."

He did not elaborate.

[Editor's Note: The shooting occurred at press time and will be fully reported next week with pictures and additional commentary from witnesses.]

IV

The Chumbleys and the Law

[A version of this story appeared in The Southern Review, Spring, 1966]

Walton walked through the morning twilight to the garage and saw that the Old Honesty padlock, the new one, was sawed cleanly in two. He looked down at the padlock for a moment, hesitant to open the door and see what was missing, when suddenly the wide door slammed into him and he reeled backwards onto the ground. Instinctively, he jammed his foot against the door and held it. The banging wasn't strong, but persistent, and all he could hear was a steady thudding against the door as something tried to push its way out. Pulling himself up to a sitting position, he scotched his other foot against the door, planting his hands behind him to brace the hold. The banging continued, and Walton sat there on the ground with the soles of his shoes flush against the door.

"Inez!" he yelled in the direction of the house: "Load my shotgun and bring it here. Hurry up!" With that, the banging stopped. Walton couldn't tell if the pressure against the door had subsided, so gradually he lessened his foothold. Then he thought he heard a sound and jammed his feet against the door again, but he could hear nothing but the squeaking hinges. "Hurry up!" he shouted to his wife again, bracing his feet more firmly against the heavy oak boards.

Then he heard a clatter of glass behind the garage and knew that the rear window had been smashed. He heaved himself up and pressed against the door with one hand and listened to the glass tinkling to the ground. He opened the door a little, and as he tried to focus through the dimness, a short, squatty figure pushed through and ducked under his arm and around the corner, disappearing into the tall ragweed behind the building. All Walton could see was a crumpled hat bobbing along the supple weeds as they closed behind the figure like water behind the stern of a fast-moving boat.

"Stop! You little sonofabitch, or I'll kill you!" Walton shouted as he hurled the large river rock that was once used to hold open the door. It hardly got past the end of the garage. When his wife got there, he blasted the shotgun into the flower-sprinkled weeds, and most of the bird shot splattered into a cluster of black-eyed Susans. They bobbed their yellow heads and smiled at him. He stood there muttering, "I'll kill 'em, ever goddam one, I tell you."

"Was it one of 'em?" she asked.

"Yeah. A young'un, I think. Ain't no old Chumbley goanna move like that."

"Was it crook-necked or regular?"

"Hard to tell, come by me so fast. Looked like a crook, way I seen its head setting up through them weeds." Walton went into the garage. The truck's gas cap was missing, and a hubcap lay in the soft dirt. He found another hubcap behind the garage amid the shattered glass. He told his wife the gas cap was gone.

"How many does that make?" she asked. He mumbled that over a dozen had been stolen altogether. He picked up a corn cob and began wrapping a rag around it and twisted it in his clenched fist until it was tight and poked it into the gas tank opening of the truck. He hammered it in securely with the heel of his hand. She watched him with her arms folded against her bosom. "Ain't no telling what else they got," she offered.

"Naw. Ain't no telling. All I know is I'm goanna have to do somethin, because they getting worse by the day. They got the mail box last night, and I've had enough of their sorry mess. Nothing left for me to do but get the sheriff." Walton studied one of the door's squeaking hinges and gently moved it back and forth. "Yeah. It's the only thing I know to do." Inez silently agreed and took the shotgun when he handed it to her. Since their telephone was out, Walton got into his truck and set off on the thirty-minute drive south to the sheriff's office.

It was after six o'clock when Walton got to the William Byrd County jail at Shaw's Pond. One deputy was on duty in the sheriff's office. He was slouched at the desk asleep. Walton waked him and told him there was some fresh Chumbley trouble in the northern end of the county and asked him to call the sheriff. He sat down and listened as the deputy picked up the telephone, called the sheriff and wearily relayed the message. When the deputy hung up, he swirled around in the chair and said, "What sort of trouble you got up there?"

"Ever kind you ever heard of," Walton said. "I ain't never seen nothin' to beat it. Them Chumbleys always been a nuisance, and they getting' bolder by the day. They got my mail box and another gas cap and some more hubcaps this morning, and my telephone ain't workin' and they mighta cut down the telephone pole again, but I ain't checked. I hope I can get the sheriff to go up there with me." Walton opened his pocket knife and began scraping on one of his fingernails.

"I hear about how sorry they all is," said the deputy. "And I'm sure glad I ain't gotta live up there around them." The deputy reached up and adjusted the knobs on the static-filled police radio. A kitchen worker came in and said he was ready for his man. The deputy walked back to the cell block and returned with a puny little Negro man walking behind him with his eyes cast to the floor. The deputy gently shoved him toward the kitchen worker and warned: "Awright, Delaware, I'm goana give you one more chance at being trusty, but if you go up there lookin' at them pretty gals again, you ain't being trusty no more." The little man nodded and shuffled after the cook into the kitchen.

"Bring us some coffee," the deputy called after them. "Yeah, Mr. Walton," he settled into the swivel chair. "I remember when they cut your phone pole down after you got your phone put in. Whatever come of that?"

"Nothin'. I told the sheriff about it but he claimed there won't nothin' he could do about it 'cause the pole they cut down's on their own land. He said he couldn't do nothin' 'til he heard from the telephone people. I know they don't have no right to cut that pole down, even if it was on their land,

but I figured if I didn't get all hot about it, things would quieten down."
Walton explained that the telephone company had erected two new poles
so that the wire went over a corner of the Chumbley property without
actually touching it with the poles.

"What got all the trouble started this time?" The deputy took a small
comb from his hip pocket and began cleaning it on his pants cuff.

"The trouble ain't really never died down from the last time," Walton
told him. "Ever since then I been missing little things here and there. Just
losing a few things in the night, but it won't never enough to worry with.
But this time, they got that mailbox and that other stuff, and I just ain't
goanna put up with it. And like I said, they might of cut that telephone line
again, but I ain't certain since I come through the short cut this morning.
Anyway, I'm goanna put the whole thing in the sheriff's hands."

"That's a sorry bunch, awright, "the deputy agreed. "But they ain't so bad
we can't take care of 'em. Last time, I reckon the sheriff figured it was sort of
up to the phone people, but you ain't goanna have to worry 'bout it this time
'cause we'll take care of it" He swooped the comb through his hair and studied
his reflection in the chrome base of the radio microphone. When the coffee
came, the deputy told Delaware it was the worst he had ever had and sent him
back to bring the whole pot and the new piece of screen. Delaware shuffled
off and returned carrying a large kettle in both hands and set it on the cold,
potbellied stove. The men poured their coffee back into the kettle, and the
deputy poured two more cups, using the new piece of screen wire to catch the
black grounds. Delaware held the screen while the deputy carefully poured the
coffee and explained that they had a new electric percolator but didn't have the
proper type of cord. They were forced to use the old prisoners' kettle.

"Ain't they mainly crook-neck Chumbleys up there?" The deputy lit
cigarette and squinted through the smoke as he flicked the match into the
empty coal box.

"Yeah," Walton looked into his coffee and barely tipped the cup from
side to side. "They got the regular-necks and the wall-eyed crook-necks,
but it's a heap more wall-eyed crook-necks than anything else. Them
crook-necks is the main trouble makers."

Both men remained seated when Sheriff Cundiff Norfleet came in
and spoke to Walton without looking at the deputy. Jerking his hand

toward the deputy, he said gruffly, "This boy here says you got some fresh Chumbley trouble up yonder. What's that bunch done now?"

"I tell you, Sheriff," Walton shook his head slowly. "I don't know what you goanna do about this. I done all I could to get along with 'em. That last time, I didn't say any more about that phone pole after the telephone people fixed it, but ever since then they been stealing me blind. Just little things mainly. You know, gas caps and hubcaps and things." Walton worked himself forward in the chair and leaned his folded arms against the heavy wooden desk and looked at the sheriff.

Sheriff Norfleet quickly shifted his hat to the other hand and backed his large rump into a waiting chair. He studied the scarred desk top briefly and looked up at Walton: "Hell, we got plenty of laws on that sort of thing, and stealing that mail box is a federal charge. They been carrying on like that long enough up there, and I guaran-damn-tee you we goanna put a stop to it this time. Hell, I'll just go up there and arrest the first crook-neck I see and lock him up on suspicion. If we have any trouble from the rest, I'll go up there and get the whole damn bunch. Which one was it in your garage this mornin'?"

"Lord, Sheriff, I don't know," Walton said. "A Chumbley's a Chumbley, and so far as I know, ain't none of 'em but the old ones got any other names. You don't hardly ever see 'em, unless they're squatted along the road. About the only time they'll get up close in the daytime is when you leave your truck parked somewhere and they come along and get in the back. That's a worrisome sort of thing, and lot of times they pretty hard to get out, and you sure don't wanta take 'em home with you."

Norfleet took a multicolored ball point pen from a plastic holder in his shirt pocket and punched it in and out. "Here's the way I figure it," he said. "We ain't got too bad a problem. All we gotta do is get a couple of the boys and go in there and arrest us a crook-neck and that ought to set things straight. That'll just let 'em know the law ain't aiming' on messin' around with 'em."

"Well, you're liable to have a devil of a time, Sheriff, but I'm leavin' the thing up to you. I don't really care about seein' any of 'em get put in jail, but I don't know what else you goanna do. I don't care too much about getting back at 'em, either, but something's gotta be done about the whole mess."

"Hell," Norfleet hoisted a fat leg onto the desk top. "They ain't many we can't handle. I know their kind, and they ain't nearly as mean as some of these people I've fooled with 'round here and I can tell you, we got some mean sonofabitches here in William Byrd County."

"I don't doubt you can't handle 'em," Walton said. "It's just that them Chumbleys ain't so mean; they mainly ornery. I reckon they mean, too, but I still don't see exactly how you aimin' on doing this thing. If you go in there and try to get your hands on them old ones, you goanna have to have an army."

"I ain't aiming on getting the old ones, particularly," Norfleet looked up. "I just figure we'll go in there and arrest one or two of 'em on suspicion and carry 'em down here and investigate 'em right good. And if that don't work, we'll just arrest some more of 'em and make sure they stay in jail awhile. It ain't goanna be no big problem. What it amounts to is making an example out of one." Norfleet picked at a worn spot on the knee of his pants.

When four deputies had trickled into the office, the sheriff explained the best approach. He would go with Walton in Walton's truck, and the deputies would go in the sheriff's car. The deputies would take the back way, circling around up there where they were building Smith Mountain Dam while Walton and Norfleet would drive up the main road, turn off, and follow the dirt road around by the Chumbley homeplace so the sheriff could refresh his mind on the geography. They would meet the deputies at Brutus Crossroads, agreeing that is would be better to keep the lawmen in the background until the best strategy could be decided. "All this really ain't necessary," Sheriff Norfleet said to Walton as they left the jail. "But it ain't no use in taking a chance."

As Walton backed the truck out of the jail parking lot, the sheriff asked, "Did you ever know that real old Chumbley? Reventon's his name, ain't it?"

"Yeah. Old Reventon. I reckon he's way over ninety, now. I been seeing him all my life but ain't ever had much to say to him. I know his grandfather was old man Chatham Chumbley, and he's the one that had all the land and money. They say Chatham was a pretty smart old fellow, but he was curious – you know, quarr, didn't fool with nobody but his own people."

Walton got out a cigarette and reached to push in the cigarette lighter and spat out a curse. The lighter was gone. "Anyway," Walton leaned into the steering wheel and struck a match. "Old man Chatham had some chillen by some of his sisters and nobody ever fooled with any of 'em since. Some folks say he had chillen by some of his own girls, but you can't always go by the way folks talk."

"I ain't got no use for them kind of people," Norfleet said as they turned off the highway and bumped down the rain-gutted road that curved along the Chumbleys' place and passed Walton's on the way to Brutus Crossroads. "I always heard old Reventon had six or seven hundred acres of land in there. How come he's held onto it?" the sheriff asked.

"Yeah, they got a right good piece of land in there," Walton rested his wrist on the shaking gear lever. "Before old man Chatham died, he seen what a sorry bunch he had raised up – you know, breedin' with his sisters and daughters and everthing. So, he got to looking' around and seen Reventon was the only one that was just about like himself, and old man Chatham figured Reventon would be the best one to keep the bunch together. So, when Chatham died, he left the main house and all the land to Reventon and said that the property had to be kept in one piece and all the Chumbleys live on it. Sorta like one of them reservations the gumint set up for the Indians."

"That's the sorriest mess I've ever heard of," the sheriff said as they began rattling down a steep hill. As Walton slowed for the curve at the bottom, the truck vibrated sharply from side to side. "And it's high time somebody did somethin' about that mess," the sheriff said, his heavy jowls joggling with the sharp shaking. "I'm tellin' you, we'll take care of 'em. You just don't go around here doing like that. We got laws against all that mess and lots of times we don't fool with it, but that whole family's illegal. We'll take care of 'em." Norfleet pushed his glasses up and loosened his belt notch.

"But like I was telling' you, Sheriff." Walton stared ahead at the road. "It ain't easy to deal with that bunch. It used to be that old Reventon didn't allow anybody to come on the place, and he did all he could to keep any of his bunch from leaving. They got enough land in there that they were able to do most everything they needed right . . . ."

"Hell! I don't care about how they got like they are," Norfleet interrupted. He tried to position himself sideways on the seat, but his corpulent leg jounced back to the floor. "All I know is there ain't no excuse for them livin' like that, and I ain't gotta understand 'em to enforce the law."

"Well, like I told you before," Walton rested his hand out of the window and looked down at the oil gauge. "I'm leavin' this whole thing up to you. Nobody's ever tried to change their ways, so I don't know what'll happen." Walton gunned the motor as he changed the gears, and orange dust seeped up through the floor boards.

"All I know about 'em is that there ain't no good in 'em," Norfleet coughed away the dust. "When did all them crook-necks get started? Where'd they come from and who in hell brought 'em here?" Norfleet heaved his left foot atop the heater box on the floor.

"Old man Chatham, the first one I ever heard anything about," Walton curled his arms around the steering wheel. "He was a regular-neck, and some of his children was too. But most of the regular-necks left home and the others kept breedin' with one another, and by the time Reventon's generation come along, most all them was crook-necks. And it was along then that the wall-eyeds started being born, and now that whole place is bustin' out with wall-eyed crook-necks."

"That's the biggest goddam mess I ever heard of," Norfleet said. "I reckon they figure the law ain't got nothing' to do with them, but we'll show 'em." They bounced along in silence until Walton pointed out where the Chumbley property began. He showed the sheriff where the telephone pole used to be that strung his wire over a corner of the Chumbley land. It had been planted just within the corner of the property line. He slowed the truck and leaned towards the sheriff to see if the new poles were down. They had been erected on either side of the Chumbley land so that the line stretched over the property without actually touching it. He finally stopped the truck.

"Ain't no poles over there," Norfleet's eyes bulged a little. "They musta chopped 'em again!" He clambered out of the truck. Walton cut the motor and followed. They sidestepped their way up the red clay bank, but Norfleet couldn't quite make it. "It's these slick office shoes," the sheriff panted as Walton helped him over the top. They found the poles chopped to the ground. The wires were cut and heavy glass insulators were missing. Walton didn't say anything, and after they had stood looking for several minutes, the sheriff spoke: "Just what I figured they done. Cut the poles. Last time, the phone people said they'd handle it, and I didn't worry too much about it, but this is right under my nose. The law ain't goanna let this pass. We'll start right in investigating who done the choppin'." Panting, Sheriff Norfleet stood with his hands on his hips.

Walton poked his foot at one of the jagged poles. "They done it awright. You can tell by the sorry choppin' that a Chumbley done it," he said as he walked the length of one of the poles and stooped to inspect the two ends of the severed line. It was a clean cut with each end coming just to the edge of a deep, V-shaped hole where an ax had slashed into the earth. "You reckon you could go look behind the front seat of my truck and bring me that tool box?" he asked the sheriff, who was hovering over his shoulder.

"What? You figure you can fix them wires back?" Norfleet asked as he righted himself and jabbed his hands into his hips.

"Yeah. I can wrap these ends back together and make the telephone work. We can call them telephone folks to come fix the poles when we go by the house." Walton looked back at the wires.

Sheriff Norfleet agreed and jerked off through the brown broom straw with one hand in his pocket and the other swinging in a wide arc by his side. Walton watched as the sheriff swished through the knee-high straw and saw him slow as he approached the bank. Then he turned and backed over the embankment and out of sight. Moments later, Walton heard a nervous, stammering yell:

"Hey Mister Walton! *Come here quick!* I got one!" Walton started for the road, and when he got to the edge of the embankment and looked down, he saw Norfleet was gripping his quivering revolver at arm's length, pointing it into the back of the truck. Squatting in the corner next to the cab was a Chumbley, a medium-sized crook-neck. Sheriff Norfleet inched his way closer to the truck, keeping the pistol pointed at the Chumbley and warning it not to move. It did not move, but squatted quietly and barely bobbed up and down.

From his position on the bank, Walton could discern that this was a grown Chumbley with a little age. The neck grew out of the trunk at a point closer to the left shoulder than to the right, and it protruded to the left at almost a forty-five degree angle. Thus, the head normally would have been located in a sideways position sort of lying on the left shoulder. But, most of the older ones had learned to cock their heads back to the right so that the whole neck was in a crook. The younger ones usually let their heads almost rest on their left shoulders. Walton was certain that this was an older one because it held its head back to the right with perfect ease. Occasionally, he had observed the younger ones trying to learn to hold their heads to the right, but they usually grew tired after a bit and let their heads flop back to the left, in their natural positions.

"If you move, I'll shoot you," the sheriff yelled as Walton stepped down the bank and walked around to the opposite side of the truck to the corner where the Chumbley was squatting. It was a wall-eyed, and Walton watched the eye flitter around in the socket while the left eye remained fastened on Norfleet and his gun.

"Look here, Chumbley," Walton said sharply. "How come you was in my garage this mornin' and what'd you do with that mail box and how come you chopped my pole down? You better tell me, or the sheriff here is going to put you in jail. Might even shoot you!"

Serenely, the Chumbley bobbled up and down, keeping the eye fixed on Norfleet. Walton looked closely at the Chumbley, trying to recognize something that might have belonged to him. The faded flannel shirt and the overalls didn't look familiar. He studied the ragged felt hat that had given up its seams to the huge head, but couldn't recall it as having been his. The breeze shifted slightly, and the Chumbley's acrid odor made Walton's nose twitch. Just then he noticed a piece of tobacco twine tied into the pocket watch loop on the front of the overalls. It dangled downward between the Chumbley's legs, and Walton moved closer until he could see clearly. On the end of the string, barely swinging, was a gas cap.

"Awright, Chumbley! That's my gas cap and you stole it," Walton raised his voice. "Gimme that gas cap!" As he reached for it the sheriff ventured closer and threatened to shoot the Chumbley. Just as Walton grasped the string, the Chumbley did a quick squat-jump to the opposite corner and the string broke. Walton examined the rusty cap and dropped it into his pocket, but the Chumbley now focused its eye on him. The bobbing became more rapid, and the walleye seemed to flitter faster as the good eye stared at Walton.

"You might as well put that gun up," Walton said to the sheriff. "It ain't goanna do no good. I told you about how Chumbleys get in your truck like this. He won't do what you tell him. Ain't but one way we goanna get him out, and that's with our hands."

"Hell, I ain't aimin' on getting him out," Norfleet said. "This looks like the one that done the choppin', and I figure I'll arrest him right here on suspicion and carry him to jail. But I tell you one thing, he don't act like no regular criminal." The sheriff fidgeted with the pistol and looked at the chunky figure that was still bobbing and watching Walton.

Suddenly, the Chumbley squat-jumped the width of the truck and held out his hand toward Walton. ""You ain't getting that gas cap back, Chumbley. You going to jail!" Walton grabbed the thick wrist with both hands. "Come here, Sheriff, and handcuff him if you want him," he said without taking his eyes from the Chumbley.

"We got him now!" Norfleet rounded the truck, loosening the handcuffs from the shiny black pouch on his belt and jangling them together. "Come on, Chumbley! Put 'em out. You the one that chopped that pole down."

The Chumbley pulled at Walton's grip briefly, and then relaxed and fixed the good eye on the sparkling handcuffs. Norfleet clanked one cuff around the wrist that Walton held. When he did, the Chumbley jiggled his forearm up and down and watched the dangling cuff clink against the side of the truck. Before either man could grab the other hand, the Chumbley heaved in a great lung full of air, and a high-pitched wheeze burst into the men's faces. Walton and Norfleet reeled backwards in the wake of what had sounded like an enormous sneeze, but recovered in time to see the Chumbley do a back flip over the side of the truck and leap up the short bank and disappear. They could hear a soft thumping and a metallic jangle moving across the field.

"Come on, let's get him!" the sheriff yelled, waiving his pistol and lunging for the bank. He jumped the ditch and started up the embankment, but his office shoes provided little traction and he fell to his knees cursing: "Goddam, I had that little sonofabitch and he got away! I was just fixing to put that other cuff on him and he sneezed and was gone before I ever knew it."

Walton leaned against the truck and watched Norfleet brushing the red dirt from his knees. "That little bastard would of been in jail before he knew it," Norfleet continued slapping at the dirt on his pants. "I almost had him and it's a good thing for him he got away. All I know is, I'm going over there to that Chumbley place and arrest ever one in sight. I'll get 'em all. Ain't no sorry Chumbley ever goanna get away from me. I've been in the business a long time, and I ain't seen one yet that could get by me. And that little bastard left here with my handcuffs. I tell you, he's goanna have to do a heap of choppin' to get *them* off!" Sheriff Norfleet shook his head in disgust and kicked a foot into one of the tires.

"Knowin' the Chumbleys," Walton said. "That rascal likes them handcuffs a heap more than plain old hubcaps and gas caps. And he wouldn't of jumped out the truck, 'cept that he probably wanted to go show 'em around. And now you seen how a Chumbley acts, how you aiming on goin' over there and arrestin' a bunch of 'em?"

"Hell, I ain't worried about that," the sheriff said. "I'll just shoot 'em if they go to resistin' arrest. I didn't shoot that one when he run, but I'll shoot the next one if I have to."

"Well, you the sheriff, but I want you to know I'm against you goin' over there and shootin' any of 'em. They just don't know no different from what they do," Walton said.

"I told you before," Norfleet said impatiently: "I don't care about what makes 'em like they are or anything else. All I know is they're goin' against the law and my job's to stop 'em."

Walton didn't answer, but started for the truck door. "I reckon you want me to take you on over to Brutus? Them boys of yours been there right long." Norfleet agreed, and as they were getting into the truck, the car carrying the deputies rounded the curve at a high speed. The column of red dust they were leading caught up with them and settled as they stopped alongside Walton's truck.

"Howdy," the driver said. "We figured y'all had probably run into a Chumbley or something."

"I reckon we *did*," Norfleet walked over to the car and folded his arms on the dusty top above the driver's window. "And he was a mean one. I had him under arrest, and the little bastard broke from me and got away with the handcuffs. I ain't never seen nothin' like it."

"Listen, Sheriff," Walton called out as he started his truck. "Like I told you, I don't want to see any of them Chumbleys get shot. Fact, I'm scared you and your boys'll go in there and make 'em so mad I'll never have peace from 'em."

"Don't you worry about that, Mister Walton. Ain't no Chumbley goanna get shot so long as they act right and don't go to resistin' and tryin' to get away and everthing." Sheriff Norfleet turned back to the deputies and began explaining his plan to go to the Chumbley place and arrest as many as he could. While Norfleet was talking, Walton noticed a red cap peeping through some vines that were clustered around a stump at the top of the bank on his right. He watched it, and its slight bobbing convinced him that it was a Chumbley, even though he could not see a face. He looked back at the sheriff and his deputies, and they were still busy making plans. Then Walton heard the vines rustling and turned around in time to see the Chumbley leap from the bank over the ditch and land in a perfect squat in the back of his truck. From the driver's seat, through the rear window, Walton could see the red baseball cap bobbing with its grimy bill pointing off to one side. It apparently was a young Chumbley, because the head lay more on the side. Walton could see also that it was a wall-eyed crook-neck, and the good eye seemed to be focused on the sheriff.

Sheriff Norfleet jerked round and drew his pistol. "Watch out, boys!" he yelled. "This is one 'em!" The deputies scrambled out of the car and flanked the sheriff with their pistols drawn. "Awright, Chumbley. You under arrest for choppin' that pole down and for general suspicion. Get out of that truck right now!" With the good eye still fixed on the sheriff, the Chumbley extended one wrist and kept bobbing. "That sonofabitch wants a set of handcuffs!" Norfleet shouted. The deputies and the sheriff moved closer. "Don't let him get away. Surround the truck!" the sheriff said nervously. "He's liable to go any minute. This one looks meaner than the last one!"

One of the deputies lunged at the Chumbley with open handcuffs and grabbed the extended wrist. He clamped one cuff about the wrist and reached for the other arm. The Chumbley squat- jumped to the other side of the truck bed and bobbed more rapidly, Sheriff Norfleet yelled, "Look out! He's fixing to jump! Shoot him if he jumps! Don't let him get away!"

At that, Walton, still in the driver's seat, jammed the truck into gear; the tires crunched into the clay-caked road. The truck shimmied for a moment, furiously spewing a cloud of orange dust over the lawmen, and roared away. The fast get-away knocked the Chumbley against the truck's tailgate, and the red baseball cap sailed over the back and disappeared in the dusty fog. As Walton spun away he heard Norfleet shout that he was going to call the federal man, because stealing the mail box was a federal violation.

Walton drove until he came to the road that led into the Chumbley place and turned in and stopped just out of sight of the main dirt road. He got out quickly, walked around and leaned both hands against the side of the truck. The Chumbley was bobbing quietly in the middle of the truck bed, staring at the chrome handcuff that was clinking against the floor. Walton realized that this was the first time that he had seen a Chumbley without a hat.

"Look here," Walton said. "I saved you from gettin' shot back there, and I want you to get outa this truck and I don't want any more trouble from any of you. You hear!" The Chumbley kept bobbing, and Walton noticed a piece of string leading into the watch pocket and suspected it was tied to another of his gas caps. *You hear!* he repeated more loudly. The Chumbley looked up, patted its head and squat-jumped over to Walton and extended its free hand. Walton took off his own ragged hat and examined it. He saw that the sweatband had come loose at the front and back. He turned his hat and looked at the bottom and top several times, and then gave it to the Chumbley.

"Now, get out of my truck, and I don't wanta see any of you anymore, or I'll call the law!" The Chumbley looked at the hat, and then jammed it onto its head. The good eye returned to the handcuff that was still clinking against the truck.

"Listen!" Walton bellowed. "Get outa this goddam truck or I'm goanna get you out with my *hands*!" The Chumbley bobbed more rapidly as he looked at the sparkling handcuffs. Then, with a great wheeze, he back flipped over the side of the truck and into the thick foliage. Walton heard him splash through the creek. That was all.

84

Later that day Walton sat with his wife on the front porch of his house. They faced the jagged, orange ribbon of a road that separated them from the expanse of the Chumbley property. He looked past the topless post at the end of the short driveway. He saw a lone crow atop the tallest tree on the horizon. It fluttered once and settled back to its post. He knew that it was the lookout, and if a single crow in the roost was shot, the others would peck the lookout to death for not sounding the warning. The crow fluttered again, and Walton could see a black blur blending into the horizon. The lone crow steadied himself on the treetop for a moment, and then followed. Walton listened for a shot, but there was none. The lookout would have another day. In the case of the crows, he thought, the law is the law, no matter what.

"Did you get things straightened out?" she asked.

"Naw," he answered absently.

V

Blood Sports

Worrying about his dog, Little Clif Jackson wallowed around in his sweaty bed sheets for almost two hours before he got to sleep. He could hear swatches of conversation from the kitchen below as his father and Emmet Adkins drank whiskey and talked about the coon-on-the-log contest the next day. Each man claimed he had the best dog, but the dog Big Clif was bragging on was supposed to be Little Clif's dog, payment for months of grueling work.

The boy could hear the tin roof popping above him as the cooler night air sucked the long day's heat from the metal and pulled squeaks from the flat-head nails that held the roof to the beams. Lying there in the late August heat, listening to the drunken argument below, Little Clif heard Emmet Adkins say to his father, "Man, you know you ain't got nothin' on my dog. I seen my dog fight a coon weighed much as he did and tear that coon all to pieces."

"Yeah," Clif said, his voice going louder and more combative. "But your dog was fightin' on dry land, and I guaran-damn-tee you he cain't touch mine fightin' a coon on a log. Hell, that dog of yours ain't got big enough feet to swim good. A good-sized coon'd swat him back to the bank with one stroke."

"Well, by God, we'll see tomorrow 'cause I hear Spittin' Sam's goana be the main coon, and ain't no dog ever got him," said Emmet Adkins. The boy leaned over the side of the bed to hear better. "And I'll tell you what else, we'll put both dogs in the match, your'n and mine, and we'll see which one's best."

"You just wastin' your money," Clif said.

"Money!" Emmet shouted. "Who's talkin' 'bout money? If my dog's best, I get your dog, and if my dog loses, you can have him unless I just flat shoot him."

About that time, Little Clif heard his mother go into the kitchen and berate her husband and Emmet Adkins for drinking and making so much noise, hollering about this and that. She usually didn't say much to her husband when he was sober, but at times, like tonight, she really cut loose on him. Sometimes the boy felt sorry for his mother who was always threatening to leave and take the boy's younger sister with her. What worried Little Clif was not that his mother would leave but that she would leave and not take him with her, reasoning that at thirteen years old, a boy should be able to take care of himself.

Little Clif's father had given him the dog, Joey, almost a year earlier in the fulfillment of a tattered work agreement they had made. The deal was that the boy would clear off the fungus growing over the surface of one of his father's irrigation ponds. The green mold completely covered the pond, making it impossible to fish and difficult to use for irrigation without clogging the irrigation pipes.

He had spent countless summer afternoons wading back and forth across the neck-deep pond. He had skimmed the slimy surface with a wide board and then beat through the bushes along the edges trying to get every speck of the thick squashy fungus. He had cut his feet and legs on sharp rocks and broken bottles and twice just missed being struck by a copperhead moccasin. It had taken the boy nearly three months of the work—but it was never to his father's satisfaction.

By the middle of July, Little Clif believed he had finished the job, but his father kept finding little pieces of fungus he had missed. He and the boy would walk along the bank, and Big Clif would spread the weeds with a long stick and show his son small splotches of fungus that were hidden by the foliage. Every now and then, during this painful ritual, Clif would say gravely: "One thing about me, Son, is I always say if you ain't goana do a job right, ain't no use doing it a-tall." Then the boy would scramble into the water and try to get out the last specks, but more always seemed to turn up.

Finally, when the pond seemed to be free of any green slime, the piles of it Little Clif had thrown along the bank had turned brown and hard. His father then insisted that the dried fungus clumps would have to be removed before the agreement could be settled. He said a good rain would wash the fungus back into the pond. So the boy set about to move the brown clumps of dried slime off the bank, but his father did not like where he had dumped it. Little Clif began to realize that his father was never going to consider the job completed.

So it was a nice surprise a few weeks later when Clif presented the boy with a black and tan coon hound pup.

"Is he really goana be mine?" he asked his father.

"Yeah, all yours," Big Clif said. The boy was overjoyed and named the dog Joey after an earlier Jackson dog that had been killed in the road. But his mother, Melba, just rolled her eyes and told the boy he was foolish to believe anything his father told him. Joey spent nights with Little Clif in the upstairs room where, during the hot nights, the tin roof pinged and popped in the heat. When Big Clif insisted that such pampered treatment would ruin a good dog, Joey moved outside and spent his nights under the house.

The boy finally went to sleep with these memories and wondering what would happen to Joey the next day at the coon-on-the-log contest. His last thoughts that night were about the real possibility that one way or another, he could lose Joey.

Little Clif woke up early and slipped out of the house without waking anyone. In the cool fresh morning, he breathed in the smell of dew and grass and damp earth as he walked down the wooden steps from the kitchen into the yard. He snapped his fingers under the house and Joey came wagging out and nuzzled into him.

"Hey there, Boy," he said to Joey as he pressed the dog's head against his thigh. Little Clif took one of the long black ears and pulled it around and wiped the sleep from the edge of the dog's eyes. They started for the barn together. The damp weeds tickled the boy's feet. When he stopped once and scrubbed his foot into the grass to stop the tickling, Joey went on ahead—his nose to the ground and his long tail wagging comfortably.

When they got to the barn, Little Clif threw out feed for the livestock and then sat down in the doorway, his feet on the cool earth. Joey sat down in front of him and curled around and began gnawing on a cocklebur lodged in his haunch.

"Listen," Little Clif said to Joey, rubbing his head. "You ain't goana like what they fixin' to do with you today, and I don't like it, but ain't nothin' I can do about it. Daddy's carryin' you over to Billy Joe Crumpton's Pond and you goana have to fight a coon on a log, and if you don't win you goana be Emmet Adkins's dog. I know you mine, but Daddy, he's actin' like you his again, and like Daddy always says, since he give you to me, he can take you away.

"Ain't nothin' I can do but hope you come out awright." The boy swallowed hard as he said that, knowing that he alone understood the peril.

Joey, who was already panting in the early heat, looked at the boy with lolling, half-closed eyes, his long tongue spilling out of one side of his mouth. Little Clif shut the barn door and started back to the house. His father, sniffling and smoking a cigarette, met them in the path. "Awright if we carry this dog over to Billy Joe's this morning, ain't it, Boy?" Big Clif said, scratching at his groin. His hat shaded his bloodshot eyes.

"Yessuh, I reckon," the boy said. "I hope he don't get tore up."

"You ain't gotta worry about this dog," Clif said, glancing over at Joey. "He's a naturally good dog, picked him out myself and he can hold his own. Get your chores done. We need to leave here before eight o'clock."

The Jackson family had been in William Byrd County in Southside Virginia for generations. Uninterested in family history, Big Clif Jackson did not know where the family had come from three generations back when they settled here as tenants on the old Sims tobacco farm called Bright Leaf. The first Jackson had been frugal and prudent in his dealings with old Jack Sims, and when a small farm came up for sale, Jack Sims was happy to help Jackson make the move from tenant farmer to land owner. It was not unusual for good people to move ahead in this fashion.

But, as sometimes happens in the nature of things, owning a little land had not sat well with the second generation of land-owning Jacksons. Frugality and prudence had slipped mightily in the scheme of their lives, and the slippage was severely acerbated by whiskey drinking which crept upon them. In fact, Clif Jackson, the boy's father, was the first in his family to openly use alcohol for anything other than an occasional spoonful for a winter cold.

"When the whiskey moves from the back of the medicine chest to under the kitchen sink, that's when the trouble starts," according to Melba Jackson, Clif's wife and mother to their two children. Growing up, Melba had never been around whiskey and struggled to keep her straight-laced parents, who lived nearby, from knowing the challenge she lived with.

As Big Clif became increasingly irresponsible, the neighbors gravely whispered the old saying, "Overalls to overalls, in three generations." Though Clif was able to make his crops and get them to market (and, to be sure, he usually dealt fairly with people), folks who knew Melba and the children felt sorry for them. The drinking had reached the point where Clif had even cooked up a strong philosophical argument for disagreeing with their preacher and made the family quit going to church. In one sense, Melba was glad because sitting in church with Big Clif could be embarrassing when he was liquored up and chose to belch out his opinions during the service. She was thankful her own parents went to a different church.

As for Big Clif's treatment of their son, Melba had made clear her disgust over her husband's treatment of the boy, his continuing teasing him over whether or not the pond job was finished. It was she who forced Big Clif to present the hound pup named Joey.

On the morning of the big event at Billy Joe Crumpton's Pond, Big Clif's truck rattled and shook going out the dirt road to the highway. He gunned the engine as they forded a shallow creek just before going up a hill to the hard road. Thrilled over getting to ride in the back of the truck, Joey's booming voice was an expression of pure joy. When they got up to the blacktop and Clif whipped the truck onto the road, Joey was knocked off balance and scrambled along the truck bed until he hit the tailgate—still booming away.

"Dog makes a helluva fuss, don't he?" Clif said.

"Gotta good voice, though, ain't he?" Little Clif said.

"Yeah, but he needs to keep his mouth shut in the water 'til he's ready to take the throat outa that coon," Clif said.

Billy Joe Crumpton's Pond was about twenty miles west of Shaw's Pond, on a road that became increasingly crooked as it ran into the low mountains and finally turned to dirt. Crumpton had been in trouble in past years with various do-gooders who objected to the cock fights he ran as well as the coon-on-the-log contests in which the ferocious fighting almost always led to the death either of the coon or the dog. Even *The William Byrd Tribune*, normally a bulwark defender of any free enterprise, had blasted the activities as "blood sports" that had been outlawed long ago. But with guidance from his lawyer, Pickeral Chumbley, Billy Joe Crumpton took refuge in the argument that such sporting events had been going on since the settlers got to William Byrd County and had never harmed anything other than dogs, coons and chickens.

They drove west with the hot early sun behind them, and the boy could see the steam rising from the night-dampened green pastures in the low grounds that ran along the Nolting River. He could see places shaded by tall poplar trees where the high grass was still damp from the night. Along the way, whites and Negroes and mules plodded along the rows of shoulder-high tobacco—the men bending and pulling the slightly yellowed leaves and stuffing them under their arms—and the mules waiting patiently at the heads of their slides, ready to pull the filled slides to the stringing place.

At the edges of fields under clumps of shade trees, mainly oaks, heavy rough boards were nailed between the trees to form bench-like shelves upon which were stacked tobacco leaves. Children stood alongside and handed leaves to the stringer, a woman whose fingers flew as she used twine to attach leaves in small bunches onto slender five-foot sticks cut from heart pine. As she whipped the leaves into bundles, the heavy green tobacco brushed her midsection leaving her dress black with tobacco gum. Her hands and the hands of the children handing the leaves to her were also black with gum. Now and then one of them would reach down for a handful of soft dirt and rub it vigorously to get rid of some of the gum.

They turned onto Brights Road that led up to Hound Hill. In the back, Joey was scrambling to keep his balance. They drove on and the boy kept looking back to see if Joey was alright. They passed a decrepit, collarless yellow mongrel with engorged teats standing along the road as if wondering what had happened to her litter of puppies. Big Clif swerved the truck toward her, hitting the shoulder of the road and barely missing the dog. "Somebody oughta shoot that sorry thing," he said.

When they got up to Billy Joe Crumpton's Pond, the man at the gate let them in free since they had a dog to enter in the coon-on-a-log contest. Joey leaned over and licked the gatekeeper as they passed through. As they got closer to the pond, the boy could hear the high, indistinct voices of women and children. He could hear squeals of laughter and the shrill call of a mother seeking a misplaced child. They rounded the last curve and heard music and saw the whole gathering—the men smoking and standing in small groups and the women and children in larger ones. Wafting smells of food made Little Clif wish he had eaten something for breakfast.

"We goana eat pretty quick," Clif announced. At events like this, Clif Jackson usually did his eating at the Hound Hill Baptist Church Booth because, as he always reminded anyone who would listen, that was the church where his first Baptism took place. They heard Homer Eanes, the master of ceremonies for the event, welcoming everyone to Billy Joe Crumpton's Eighth Annual Coon-on-the-Log Contest. Homer was wearing a baby-blue leisure suit, blue shirt, Texas string bowtie and white cowboy hat. A dab of pink stomach showed through where a button had given away.

Little Clif's attention was diverted when Joey spotted a dog he knew and tried to scramble away to greet him. The boy jerked Joey back and began looking around himself to see who he might know. With the heat rising, the crowd was churning slowly, and Little Clif saw Emily Thomas and some other children he was in school with.

Then Homer Eanes started talking about the prayer: "And now, ladies and gentlemen, I am going to turn the program over to Deacon Flournoy Bobbitt of the Clustered Congregation Independent Church to let the lord know of our gratitude for his many blessings." Deacon Bobbitt mounted the stage and raised his hands and tilted his head back and prayed vigorously.

Just then, Little Clif spotted his father off in the crowd talking to Emmet Adkins. Even from a distance, he could tell that Emmet was already drinking whiskey. The sure sign was when Emmet began to cock his head over to the left as he talked. The boy watched them for several minutes and then saw the men head off into the woods where, he figured, they had a stash of whiskey.

The boy went back and sat with the dog on the tailgate of the truck for a few minutes and then got a piece of rope and tied Joey to the truck and went off to look around. It would be another hour or so until the contests started. On his way down to the pond he saw the holding pen with the coons and went over to look at them. He liked coons and enjoyed going down to the creek near his house to put bread on the bank. Then he would lie in the brush in the early morning and wait for a coon to come along and discover the bread. Often the coon would take the bread in his paws and wash it in the water. As he washed it, the bread would disappear, and the puzzled coon would squat there watching the particles float down the creek.

Here at Billy Joe's, Little Clif stood close to the cage and watched the coons. There were about a dozen of them. Most were sleeping, but two were wrestling. Standing on their hind legs like bears, they fell into each other and weaved back and forth and then finally toppled into furry bundles of black and brown and white. An older and much larger coon watched the two youngsters wrestling, shifting his gaze back and forth from the wrestlers to the boy. That coon, Little Clif figured, must be Spittin' Sam. He had only one ear, and his left front paw was badly mangled; he could see the distinct hairless scar left from the teeth of a steel trap. In addition to that, some of the coon's claws had been chewed off. Little Clif shook the wire of the cage to see what the old coon would do. The younger ones stopped wrestling and scampered to the far side. Spittin' Sam didn't move but lay there looking at the boy.

"Awright, young fella, now you jest move along," said a friendly voice behind him. It was Billy Joe Crumpton himself. "We goana move these coons down by the water and get 'em all stirred up, poke 'em with sticks, give 'em a taste of what they got comin'. You can come help, if you wanta?"

"No," the boy stammered. "Gotta go find somebody right now." Already, the younger coons were looking at Billy Joe Crumpton and hissing and cowering as if they knew him—all but Spittin' Sam who didn't move.

As Little Clif walked through the crowd that was settling down to some serious eating, his thoughts were squarely on Joey who had no idea he faced being torn to pieces by Spittin' Sam, or becoming known as a coward for the rest of his life. But the worst part for Little Clif was thinking about how lonely his life would be without his companion.

About that time, he ran into Emily Thomas who asked about Joey and offered her commentary: "I think it's awful!" she said. "I mean, it's mean to the coons and mean to the dogs, and some of these people get to drinking liquor, and Momma says we goana leave early because some of these people might get to fightin'. We just come 'cause of our church booth. Momma, she says the only thing good about any of it is these drinkin' people do go to eatin' and buyin' stuff and that helps our church."

"I know what you mean," the boy said, glancing around to see if his father was nearby. He cringed at the thought of Emily seeing Big Clif drunk with Emmett Adkins.

"Like I always tell Momma," Emily went on. "It's awful to kill them dogs and the coons, and that ol' Billy Joe Crumpton, Daddy says sooner or later, he's goana get in trouble over this thing and all the chicken fights he runs. I don't care that much about the chickens, but I feel sorry for the coons and dogs. How come you bring your dog up here?'"

"Well, it's what my daddy wants to do, and he give me the dog and like he says, if he give him to me, he can take him away...."

"*Woo-Wee!*" the girl laughed. "You better think again on that one. I mean, if you give somebody something, then you done GIVE it to them. They cain't go and take it back."

"That's sort of what my momma says, but Daddy, he sees it different, and nothin' I can do about it."

Little Clif meandered down to the water where several men were poking the caged coons and hollering at them. Others were there with their dogs trying to get them riled up. Billy Joe Crumpton, using a long-handled pincer device, extended it down through a trap-door in the top of the cage and snagged one of the smaller coons across its shoulders just behind its front legs. The coon thrashed about mightily while another man flipped a thin metal cable with a slip-knot over its head and wrenched it tight. They then dropped the coon into a burlap bag and took the bag to a rowboat. The anchored log was about fifty feet offshore with a clasp sunk in the middle to which they attached the coon's chain. Then, as the men pushed off a few feet from the log, the coon wriggled from the bag and onto the log. There, he was tethered with enough chain to move end-to-end on the log. If he slipped from the log, he had about three feet of slack that enabled him to maneuver in the water.

The point of the contest was for a dog to swim out and to attack and kill the coon. Or the coon might kill the dog. Most anything could happen, especially if the coon went after the dog in the water. Some dogs, to the shame of their owners, swam out, saw what they faced, and quickly returned without an encounter. As for the coon, he usually stayed on the log until he was ripped to pieces and killed. A rare survivor was Spittin' Sam who was in his fourth year at the contest.

By this time, bedlam had broken out on the shore where all the dogs, each held by its owner on a line, were in high salute. Some were baying, others howling and young dogs like Joey sort of yipping nervously. Little Clif did not see his father or Emmet Adkins, and as far as he knew, Joey was still tethered to the truck. For once, he hoped his father and Emmet Adkins would become so occupied with drinking in the woods that they would forget about the contests.

When it was clear the first contest was about to begin, Little Clif started back to the truck to check on Joey. On the way, he saw his father and Emmet Adkins standing a little ways off the path. Big Clif was actually turning up a pint bottle when Little Clif saw him. He hurried on, hoping the men had not seen him. Joey was asleep in the truck bed up toward the cab where he had found some shade. Little Clif brought him some water and rubbed his long ears. "Joey, it's bad what's fixin' to happen, and all you done is be a good dog and a good friend." A panting Joey pushed his head into the boy's legs. Little Clif's lips faintly trembled as he thought about how much he loved his dog.

Then, to avoid his father, he took a different route back to the pond where the day's main event was getting underway.

Two men were rowing back to the shore from chaining the first coon to the log. The young coon paced the length of the log, pawing at the chain on its neck and looking from side to side at the water. His shiny wet-black nose twitched as he waddled along, occasionally stopping and looking at his wavering reflection in the water. The log steadied and he stopped and gingerly pawed at his reflection but quickly withdrew his foot when it dipped into the water.

Then the first dog started out toward the log. He paddled clumsily, splashing and sneezing and beating his front legs frantically, but making his way in the right direction. The dog's head was erect, his nose held high, but by the time he got to the log he was panting hard and taking in water and coughing it back. He didn't slow to circle the log but started clambering on to it as soon as he got there. His front feet hooked over the log, he clung there gasping. The coon moved into him, swatting and clawing, its small mouth snapping its sharp little teeth. The dog beat his legs several times and tried to bark but began choking and slid back into the water. But as he slid, one of his feet caught the chain that was around the coon's neck and the coon tumbled into the water, floundering as helplessly as the dog he was now entangled with. The men on the bank roared their approval. The coon held his head straight up to keep it out of the water, and the dog thrashed straight into his neck, ripping it open. The coon struggled for a minute or so and then floated gasping at the end of the chain. The greenish water turned black with blood. The dog started for the coon again, but began choking and retreated to the log and pawed at it until the men in the boat rowed out and pulled him aboard.

Little Clif looked over to where they had brought in the dead coon. A crowd had gathered around, and he heard several men laughing jubilantly. He guessed that they had won their bets. He looked out at the fresh coon that was now pacing the length of the log, pawing at the log and shaking its head.

The boy started down toward the water where they kept the fresh coons before sending them out to the log, and he heard Homer Eanes announcing that the main feature of the day was going to be Rube Mitchell's dog. Homer Eanes said that Rube Mitchell's dog had been in the last four contests and had never lost. Little Clif knew the dog—a hulking crossbreed of German shepherd and hound.

Homer Eanes said that the coon Rube Mitchell's dog was going to fight—Spittin' Sam, was the meanest and fightingest coon in William Byrd County. Three years earlier, Spittin' Sam had stepped into a claw-toothed steel trap along the Nolting River on Kate Sims's Bright Leaf farm. His considerable size—well over twenty pounds—made him of great interest to Billy Joe Crumpton who, when he heard, went straight away and managed to get Sam out of the trap without killing him. At last year's contest, said Homer Eanes, Sam put on the best show anyone could remember and still held his position on the log after numerous attacks. He had killed three dogs and mangled four. Others retreated before the encounter.

But Rube Mitchell's dog and Sam never met last year, and this was to be the major match of the day. Neither creature had ever been beaten, and the betting was going strong both ways.

When Little Clif got down to the holding box, two middle-sized coons were cowering in one corner. The big one-eared coon, Spittin' Sam, was curled near the door of the box with his eyes fixed on two men with heavy gloves who were opening the small door. The white around Sam's face was not sharply distinguishable from the rest of his head because of the gray hair mixed in with the black. An old wrought-iron metal collar—seemingly hand-forged--was fastened around his thick neck. A small ring had been welded to it so that a small chain or wire could be inserted into the ring without having to deal too closely with the coon. One of the men reached in with the pincers and tried to grab Sam and quickly jerked back, though Sam had only looked at him. There was some laughter and a curse. The other man got one prong of the pincers under the iron collar and hoisted Sam up by the neck so the chain could be attached. Sam gently pawed at the chain with his good foot. The men pulled Sam down toward the water and lifted him by the chain and deposited him into a cage at the bottom of the boat. Sam choked and coughed as the chain strangled him but offered no frenzied resistance.

"That there's a thinkin' coon," said one of the men. "Savin' his strength."

On the way back to his spot on the bank, Little Clif saw Rube Mitchell's big dog tied to a truck. Rube was rubbing the dog's gray muzzle into the carcass of a coon that had just been brought in. The dog's hackles were bristling along his back as his master jammed his nose into the coon's bloody throat.

By the time the boy got back to his watching spot, he could hear the commotion starting as people cheered Rube's dog. The dog's deep barking drowned out the yipping of the others waiting their turns—the ones that hadn't yet had their muzzles rubbed into a bloody coon carcass. Rube Mitchell was pounding his dog on the back and yelling and pointing at the log bobbing in the water. Little Clif looked out at Spittin' Sam. The big coon had settled into the middle of the log and was looking toward the excited crowd on the bank. From where the boy stood, Sam looked motionless with his mangled paw tucked under his body.

With a shove from his master, Rube's dog lunged into the water and beat as frantically as the others, but he moved faster because of his big feet. Sam seemed to shift his weight as he watched the dog approaching, but he still did not rise to his feet. Rube's dog slowed as he approached the log—the critical point when some dogs executed a circular retreat. This dog seemed committed and attempted a strong guttural snarl, but he began choking and coughing. He was almost to the log when Sam rose to his squatty height, head low and hind quarters high. The dog circled to the other side of the log and Sam slowly turned, keeping his face to the dog that had started an approach to one end. Sam lumbered to that end, crouching and facing the dog. He stood up as the dog almost reached the log, but his mangled paw got caught in the chain. He shook his paw loose from the chain just as the dog began clambering onto the end of the log. Moving low and slow, Sam retreated to the other end of the log. The dog slipped in the slime at first but when he found his footing, he started down the log for Sam. The log was slick with blood and entrails. When the dog was about halfway along the log, he slipped, straddling the log and clutching it so he wouldn't roll back into the water.

Sam started in low and fast and straight for the dog's face. The dog kept snarling and barking, but the pitch was higher as he tried to hold on to the log, his front feet beating in the water. Sam hit him hard and head-on. The dog's barks turned to piteous yips as the coon tore into his face and eyes, ripping at him with his teeth and his good foot as he tried to get to the throat. But the dog had flattened his head against the log, and as Sam tore away at his face and eyes, the dog jerked his head up and clamped his teeth into the coon's underside. The coon flipped to one side but caught himself with his good paw and dangled halfway in the water. The dog tried to lunge forward and sideways into Sam's head, but as he did so he gave the coon a clear shot for his throat. Sam heaved upward and slashed his teeth into the tender gray underside of the dog's neck.

The dog scrambled wildly and then slowly went limp. Little Clif could see the dog's blood spreading across the log and soaking the coon's head. Sam was still in the water, clutching to the log with his good foot. He pulled himself up onto the log and limped to one end, looking back and keeping his eyes on the bleeding and wheezing dog draped over the middle of the log. A flap of bloodied skin hung from the coon's chest and underside. The mangled paw was bloody, and Sam held it against his bloody chest. The dog tried once to raise his head, but it dropped back to the log and he slowly slid into the dark water. Sam settled into a crouch and watched the dog bobbing in the water. Sam didn't lick his wounds but kept watching as the dog began to sink. He then turned to face the men who were rowing out to get Rube Mitchell's dog.

On his way up the hill to the truck, Little Clif met his father and Emmet Adkins. A glance told him they were plenty drunk and had heard enough from Homer Eanes over the loudspeakers that they were ready to put their dogs up against Spittin' Sam. Big Clif was dragging Joey by the rope around his neck, and the boy heard his father say, "Homer Eanes might be able to dance with a fiddle, but he don't know shit about dogs and coons. That damn Sam ain't goana out-think no dog of mine."

"Hey, Boy!" Clif hollered when he saw his son. "Where the hell you been. We ate while ago and didn't see you nowhere. Go find Emmet's boy and tell him to get that dog ready to fight."

"And tell 'at little scannel he better get his tail over here!" hollered Emmet Adkins. "Tell Junior I said to get my dog over here and tell him that if he don't win it's goana be his tail. Now you tell Junior that's what I said." The men were drunk enough to be frightening to Little Clif as he took off running down to the coon box where he had last seen Emmet's boy Junior.

He found Junior Adkins by the boat that had just brought in the carcass of Rube Mitchell's dog. A crowd of men and boys were standing there saying they found it hard to believe that after so many wins, Rube's dog was dead at the teeth of an old coon with a mangled foot. Several said that luck had just run out for the dog. Others swore that Sam was getting smarter in his old age and that he didn't out-fight the dog; he out-figured him. But they declared that their own dogs were not going against Sam, and Junior Adkins was standing there agreeing with them.

About that time, Junior Adkins's older sister, a scrawny teenager with a pimply face and a sad little denim-wrapped backside, came over to see what was going on. "If y'all ain't goana send the dog out to get him," she said. "Somebody better shoot that old hateful coon." She stomped off up the hill. "I just hate them old coons," she muttered.

"Listen!" Little Clif said sharply to Junior. "Our daddys're up there drunk, and yours says you better get up there with your dog 'cause they fixin' to send him against Sam."

"Hell, he's crazy to send him out there," Junior said, echoing the others. "That's a thinkin' coon. But it's his dog and I ain't got nothin' to do with it, but somebody needs to kill that nasty old coon. Look at him just settin' there lookin' at us." Sam was still crouched on the log, slowly shaking his mangled paw and bleeding lightly from the furry pink slab that hung from his chest. The coon faced the men on the bank who were examining Rube Mitchell's dog with the gaping hole in his throat.

Sounds of hollering and stomping burst from the bushes up the bank, and Little Clif saw his father and Emmet coming toward him, arguing furiously and dragging Joey along with them. Clif gave Joey a kick once when he tried to make a full stop only to be pulled along on his haunches. "Come on! You goddamn sorry dog," Clif yelled. "Ain't no damn coon goana out-smart no dog of mine."

Several men and women started gathering up their children and someone spoke of getting the sheriff to come do something about Emmet and Big Clif. But most folks were egging them on, taunting them to send out their dogs.

Emmet had sent his boy Junior up the hill to fetch their dog, and he was back with a boney, trembling hound that was in about the same condition as Joey. Junior was jerking him along with a rope around his neck. Big Clif and Emmet were set to let the dogs go, and then someone suggested that they let Little Clif and Junior flip a coin to see which dog went first. There were cheers from the bystanders, as Lady Luck called on Junior Adkins to go first.

They started down to the waterside to turn the Adkins dog onto Sam, and in the hub-bub, Clif dropped the rope that was tied to Joey's neck. The moment he was free, the dog took off straight for Little Clif, his tail set firmly between his legs. At first the dog whimpered and rubbed his nose into the boy's legs and pushed against him. Then he became calmer and started licking the boy and whining in that high nervous pitch that comes just before a rabbit yelp. Little Clif rubbed the dog's nose and ears and looked away so no one would see the tears welling up in his eyes. "There just ain't nothing' I can do," he mumbled to Joey. "You goana have to go after that coon and there ain't no way out of it. Best thing for you is to swim out there and turn around and come back. It don't matter to me if they say you yellow." The dog continued to nuzzle into the boy, whining and whimpering, seeking refuge where there was none.

When Little Clif started down to the water to watch Emmet's dog, Joey stayed right beside him, still whining. Emmet's dog kept trying to get away from the water, and Emmet kept pushing him toward it. Some of the men were laughing at the spectacle, but all were encouraging Emmet to make the dog perform. Spittin' Sam was in his same position—facing the pond bank. His head now rested on his front feet. The water around the log was calm.

Finally, Emmet Adkins angrily picked up his dog and hurled him into the water, and the dog started for the log. He beat the water like all the others but seemed to move with more regularity. Sam didn't move as the dog approached. But before he even got close enough for the bloody water to spray up pink, the dog began to make a wide arc. Emmet's dog circled and started for the shore at a point well below where the men were standing. Cursing and hollering, Emmet lunged along the shore to retrieve the dog when he came ashore. The dog seemed to be making a clear attempt at staying out of Emmet's way, and soon all the jeering crowd could hear was an occasional yelp or a curse or a splash.

Then the crowd started hollering for Clif to get his dog ready, and Little Clif could feel Joey go tense and begin quivering as his father started coming towards them. Little Clif rested his hand on Joey's head as his father came up. "Listen, Daddy," the boy said. "The dog's scared and we don't want him to do like Emmet's dog done. Let me send him out there. He ain't so scared when I'm foolin' with him."

Big Clif stood wobbling a little from the shoulders up and then said, "I don't give a goddamn who sends him out there. I just don't want my dog doing like Emmet's dog done. If this here dog turns yellow on me, I'll kill him myself, you *hear that, Boy!*" Clif was shouting and waving his arms, and the crowd was laughing and urging him on.

"Tell it like it is, Clif!" someone yelled.

"Your dog can do it!" another yelled.

The boy could feel Joey tighten all over, flinching slightly from the loud harsh words. He untied the rope and dropped it on the ground, resting his hand on the dog's head and walking toward the bank. Little Clif wasn't speaking or smiling, and the raucous commotion of the crowd seemed to subside. It was one thing to torment a drunken fool like Big Clif Jackson, but not quite the same with a boy and his dog. Probably from sheer terror, Joey seemed less tense and even a little jaunty. Little Clif hoped desperately that Joey would do anything except what Emmet's dog had done. He wanted him to at least go out there and get swatted before retreating. And he didn't want his father to go chasing around the pond hollering and cussing trying to get his dog to come back. And, of course, there was the possibility that Clif would kill Joey himself if he behaved as a coward.

"Good luck, Boy," came a nice voice from the crowd. Little Clif did not look to see who had spoken, but then a familiar voice reached his ears.

"All y'all oughta be ashamed," said Emily Thomas from Little Clif's sixth grade class. "Cussing and drinking and killing God's creatures!" Looking right at Little Clif, she shook her head in disgust. Emily's words brought together what Little Clif had been thinking all day. Everyone here loved dogs. Most people at least respected the raccoon as an interesting and sometimes comical part of rural life. So where did the idea come from for these cruel and bloody fights? Or was the real truth that somewhere deep in man's soul there lurked a desire to maim and kill?

When they got to the water's edge, Little Clif stooped down and shouted, "Awright, Boy! Sick him!" He whacked Joey across his flank and gave him a shove into the water. Joey tread water for a few seconds, head straight up, and then got his bearings and went directly for the log. Sam did not move but lay there facing the dog beating his way toward him. The sun had sunk low and was behind Sam, making him look like a thick black knot, or a large turtle on a floating log. And because of the sun, all the water splashed up by the dog was pink and red and orange, clouding the view from the bank. Earlier it had been easy to see just what was happening, but now everything was in silhouettes, dark against the bright evening sun. Joey was getting closer, but his erect head looked like a small black object moving toward a larger one—both engulfed in a mist of orange and red, sometimes flashing green and blue. Still, the black knot was motionless. Joey moved straight into the log and there were several frenzied moments of splashing with the spray going higher and nobody could see anything. Within a minute, everything had settled and the colored spray had turned to a hazy mist hanging over the scene. But it was clear that Joey was hanging on to the side of the log. It was impossible at first to tell whether the dog had the coon or the coon had the dog. The men

103

rowed out and let Little Clif go with them. They found Joey clutching the side of the log with his teeth firmly embedded in Sam's throat.

When the boat returned to shore, Little Clif and Joey were riding in the front and the boy, his face split with a huge grin, was holding up Sam's carcass for all to see. Big Clif was standing on the bank and as the boat pulled in he grabbed the dead coon from the boy and started yelling. "I told y'all I had the best dog, and I'm goana find that goddamned Emmet Adkins and rub his nose right in this dead coon!" Holding Sam by his thick ringed tail, Clif crashed into the bushes following the same route Emmet had taken.

Little Clif heard Homer Eanes prattling that if there is anything better than a fighting dog, it's a thinking dog, and that somehow Little Clif Jackson's dog had out-figured Spittin' Sam. Homer Eanes called for folks to bring Little Clif and his dog up on the stage to be recognized.

"Ladies and gentlemen, let's tell Little Clif Jackson how proud we are of him and his dog Joey!" There was some clapping, and the boy reached down and rubbed the dog's neck. Joey did not have a sign of a scratch on him, and stood panting with his long tongue hanging from his mouth.

A few minutes later, Big Clif staggered up to the bandstand, steadying himself by leaning his elbow on the edge. He still held Spittin' Sam whose carcass had bloodied his pants leg. "You get the hell down here, Boy!" he yelled at Little Clif. "You ain't got no business being up there claiming all the glory about what my dog done!"

"Well, looka here, folks, we got Mister Clif Jackson here, too, and he's daddy of Little Clif and Joey," Homer Eanes told the crowd. "Come on up here, Clif, and say a few words to the folks about how you trained this fine dog."

"Hell, naw!" hollered Big Clif. "I ain't comin' up there showin' my ass and makin' a fool of myself." This was met with laughter among the people still standing around the bandstand. Little Clif glanced around and saw his friend Emily Thomas being pulled away by her mother. "Boy, come on the hell on down here, we gotta go!" Clif was weaving on his feet as Little Clif hopped off the platform. Joey followed, boldly sniffing the coon carcass.

When they got to the truck, the first thing Big Clif did was to tie Spittin' Sam to the hood ornament. He made Joey sit in the front between him and the boy. As soon as he settled behind the steering wheel, Clif reached under the seat and pulled out a pint of store-bought whiskey called "1889."

"Now Son," he said. "We done good today, and this dog done real good killin' that coon, so I think we all oughta have a swallow and then we'll start for home. You old enough to learn to enjoy a little swallow now and then the way I do."

"Yessir," the boy said, relieved over the gentle tone from his father. "But I dunno how we'll give Joey any?"

"Maybe we'll just get him a hotdog, but you go ahead now and take a swallow. Ain't gotta chaser here but you need to learn to drink without a chaser 'cause lot of times you drinkin' somewhere where ain't nobody got a chaser."

"I wouldn't mind a hotdog myself," Little Clif said. "Where's Mister Adkins?" He instantly regretted that he raised the subject.

"Never could find the sonofabitch. Hope he fell in the pond and drowned. He's as sorry as that damn dog of his. Hurry up, and take your swallow," Clif said, shaking his hand toward the bottle the boy was holding.

The boy took a small draw of the hot, stinking liquid, and his empty stomach retched in rebellion. He muffled a deep gag. He had had nothing to eat since supper last night. Clif reached for the bottle and took a long swallow, let out a raucous whoop, took another quick swallow and handed the uncapped pint back to Little Clif. Joey leaned over and gave Big Clif a sloppy lick across the face, and the man slammed his elbow into the dog who yelped and leaned into the boy.

"Goddamn!!!!" Big Clif hollered. "Man, what a day! Just look at that damn old coon layin' there, and my dog dunnit!" Jubilant now, he started the truck and jammed it into reverse and stomped the gas so hard that red dust from the wheels spinning in reverse enveloped the truck and filled the cab. Then Clif hit a forward gear, stomped the gas again, and they were off—spinning and speeding along the dirt road, fish-tailing in the curves. Clif blasted his horn as they flew through the entrance gate, the dead coon sliding all over the hood. Little Clif hung on to Joey as they were both thrown around in the cab. Clif was hunched over the steering wheel, grinning madly, and when he finally approached the paved road he hollered, "Now we goana see what this truck will do!" The tires squealed as they tore into the pavement.

Just then the capless whiskey bottle flew out of Little Clif's hand and hit the floor, spilling the whiskey, its odor filling the cab. Joey faced the open window, enjoying the breeze, and then Clif locked the brakes and slid to a stop sideways in the road. Joey and the boy slammed into the dashboard and windshield.

"Catch that bottle, Boy!" he yelled, pointing to the floorboard. "That's all we got left!" Little Clif retrieved the bottle while it still had an inch of whiskey in it and handed it to his father who polished it off and tossed the bottle out the window. "Now, Boy, you hold onto that dog, now, and don't let him be flying all over the truck like that. Might hurt him."

"Yessir," the boy said. "I don't want nothin' to happen to Joey. He was lucky today."

"*Lucky!*" Big Clif said hooting the word twice. "It won't *luck*! Better not be, 'cause that dog's the new grand champion, and he's goana have to fight ever year to keep his title. So hang on to him tight!"

Big Clif Jackson put the truck in gear, stomped the gas and tore off toward Shaw's Pond. Blood from Spittin' Sam was now splattering onto the windshield. Leaning over the steering wheel, his eyes squinted, his mouth pursed, going faster and faster and faster, taking curves on the inside, clipping a mailbox, Big Clif was squalling with pure joy. When the boy last looked, the speedometer reading had just passed one hundred miles an hour. Little Clif hugged Joey as hard as he could and buried his face into the fur of the panting dog's neck.

VI

The Bright Leaf Waltz

From her chair by the window, Kate Sims looked across the dimly lit parlor. Something was out of order on the mantelpiece. She thought it was one of her long black leather gloves draped over the edge. But it was summertime, and Emma was supposed to have put the winter garments away in the attic. *Looks like Emma would've learned by now,* she thought.

Miss Kate looked away, out the front window and down the long dirt road that cut through the rolling green tobacco fields and past the graveyard and across several miles of Bright Leaf, her family's old tobacco plantation. Off to her left in the distance, along the southern boundary of the place, was the tree line of the Nolting River where her forebears had operated a gristmill. Near there, just up the hill from an ancient rocky ford in the river, the old road connected to the rest of the world.

Kate Sims had little interest in the rest of the world, preferring the easy company of her dreams and the memories of those she had loved and hated during her eighty-five years. Some days she most enjoyed the soft memories, but more often she delighted in resurrecting hard memories of old enemies, long ago subdued and dead. *That's another thing nice about the dead,* she enjoyed saying. *They don't argue with you.*

Among the revered figures in her mind was Captain Jackson Sims, her father, who taught her how to raise and cure bright leaf tobacco, to train horses and keep the books in order. As the youngest of his children, Miss Kate, as she was called, had a special place with him. Early each day, Captain Jack went to the pantry with a drinking glass and prepared his mixture of a little whiskey, a little water, a little sugar, a little more whiskey. He'd briskly stir the concoction. Just as he put the glass to his lips, he would hand little Katie the spoon for her to lick. It was her special privilege, an anchor in Kate Sims' childhood memories.

But all that was gone. Now Bright Leaf's tobacco acreage was leased out to a man with a name from somewhere else. Gone were the old faces and long-ago voices of the field hands. The only workers who passed along the road spoke a high, happy-sounding Spanish. When the Mexicans first started coming to work in the tobacco, they wore big wide-brimmed straw hats that Miss Kate enjoyed seeing bobbing in the ocean of waving green leaves. But now they all wore the same soiled, squnched-down baseball caps that had taken the countryside like a plague.

What a good old hot summer day, Miss Kate thought as she pushed aside the long window curtain and picked up a jelly glass filled with whiskey. She took a little swallow and put the glass back behind the curtain. *Yes*, she thought, as the whiskey tingle danced across her shoulders, *nothing like a good old hot summer day*. It was late morning, and she wished she had not agreed to see Bobby Barksdale from the bank to discuss what he called "estate planning." She knew that was but a fancy term for trying to get at her money.

Miss Kate turned away from the window, and her eyes again fell upon the mantelpiece. A flush of irritation swept over her. She squinted hard at whatever was hanging over the side. She got up from her chair and crossed the room to see what had intruded upon the field of little treasures that lived upon the mantle shelf. It did not make sense that what she saw were really her nice leather gloves.

She stood eye-level with the top of the mantel and reached for the offending item. Instinctively, her hand stopped and then slowly drew back. She saw that the part hanging over the edge was attached to something more serious.

"*God-a-mighty*" she said softly. Before her eyes were not gloves at all, but the tail end of a long, heavy-bodied black serpent draped across the width of the mantelpiece. Quietly and slowly, she moved to her left until she could see its head. She glanced back along the mantel and puzzled over how the snake had made its way through the little pieces of china and crystal. It wound along the elegant bell jar that held her father's pocket watch, as well as the display of buttons from her great grandfather's uniform that he wore during the War Between the States. The snake's body rested on the edge of the small gold music box from Tiffany's that featured the delicate crystal figure of a bejeweled ballet dancer. The piece was a former husband's family heirloom, considered very valuable by his family, who had once hired a lawyer to retrieve it.

Closer inspection revealed the snake's leathery, off-black texture. *It's an old snake,* Miss Kate figured. *And it's a quiet snake and a long snake.*

Now, face-to-face with the blunt nose of the motionless creature, Miss Kate looked at its still, amber eyes. She wondered for a moment whether it was dead or alive. Then the forked tongue flicked out.

"Emma!" she shouted, drawing back. "Come get this snake! *Right now!"*

At the other end of the house, back past the center hall, on the other side of the kitchen in the pantry, a small, broad-bottomed woman, the last Negro at Bright Leaf, could hear Miss Kate yelling. Emma couldn't understand what her mistress was saying, but she knew it was urgent. She pulled on her shoes and got up creakily from her chair. Emma had lived on the place for all of her eighty-two years, most of that time here in the main house. Emma knew as much about Kate Sims as anyone alive. She knew almost as much as Miss Kate herself.

"Goddamit, Emma, where are you!" Miss Kate came into the kitchen as Emma emerged from the pantry.

"Lord, Miss Kate, what in the world's the matter?" Emma could tell Miss Kate was agitated. Her dull gray eyes were alive, her mouth pursed. Her distinctive lower lip, a family trademark remindful of the elephant's tender little protuberance at trunk's end, was in full pout.

"There's a big old snake in the parlor! Layin' across the mantel!"

"Aw, Miss Kate, now you know ain't no snake on the mantel. You sure this ain't another one them dreams you get ever now and then? Ain't no way no snake can get up on the mantel."

"I don't know how he got up there, but that's where he's at," Miss Kate said. "Coulda come down the chimley and crawled right around. I don't know, but I want that damn snake off my mantel!"

"Yassum! Want me to go get our hoe? That's the best thing for a big old snake, a good sharp hoe!"

"Naw, if we take the hoe to him, he'll get to fightin' and whippin' around and break everything up there."

"Lord, that's right, Miss Kate," she mumbled, putting her hand to her mouth.

Slowly, they went back through the main hall, two old ladies in ancient lockstep, and slipped into the parlor. Now, the serpent had moved its tail slightly so that it was no longer draped over the edge. The tail was now nudged up against the bell jar that held Captain Jack Sims's gold pocket watch.

"Lord, what a snake that is," whispered Emma. She moved a little closer toward the tail end, watching so that the amber eye on her side could not see her. "Lordy me, Miss Kate, looky yonder. I do believe that snake done just ate. He be here awhile takin' it easy."

Miss Kate peered closer to see the distinct lump Emma pointed to about midway along the snake's body. "Sure enough, you're right, Emma. He musta ate just 'fore he got here, probably a baby rabbit or sumpin."

"Could be one of our big rats," Emma offered.

"We don't have rats like that around here," Miss Kate said.

"Yassum, but I tell you this, Miss Kate. That's one sly old snake, now ain't he? Eat hisself a big dinner and then come up here in this cool parlor and go to sleep. Yes ma'am, that's a sly old snake. Big'un, too"

"Oh, for God's sake, Emma!" Miss Kate whispered harshly. "That snake don't know what he's doin'! He's just a damn snake."

"Yassum, but look like he got *us* foxed pretty good," Emma said. "Him layin' up here in the cool parlor with a full belly and us don't know what to do about him."

Miss Kate motioned for Emma to follow her from the parlor into the center hall and then gently closed the door. "Awright," she said. "How we goana get him out?"

"And jest when we got company comin'."

"*Who's* comin'?" Miss Kate demanded.

"Remember, you know that nice Mister Bobby Barksdale from the bank at Shaw's Pond? He comin' after while, so I reckon y'all'll wanta set in the livin' room since that snake is usin' our parlor?"

"That'll be awright," Miss Kate said. Pensive now, sweat breaking slightly on her wide brow, Miss Kate's gray eyes narrowed and the Sims lip poked out. "We have to do somethin' about that snake," she said. "There used to be folks around could get snakes off mantels, but I 'spect they about all gone. Ole man George Lowe, he was good at it, but he's dead. What happened to that old crazy man over at Scuffleton, claimed he can make bears dance?"

"You mean that fella they say's a Catholic? Karewski or sumpin?" Emma said. "Fellow fixes shoes? He ain't at Scuffleton, Miss Kate. He stay at Bog Town and I believe he dead."

"Well, maybe we better call and check on him."

"Now, Miss Kate, what you want me to serve that nice Mister Barksdale?" Emma said. "I 'spect sumpin cool, on a hot day like this?"

"Emma, we need to talk about this snake, but you just bring Mister Barksdale a cold Coca-Cola. And don't go to talkin' and carryin' on with him like you do sometimes. You know about those Barksdales when they get all stirred up, and we don't need any of that around here."

"Lord," Emma said. "I reckon I do know about them Barksdales. I can tell you...."

"*Emma!* Don't you start on that! I don't want to hear *nothin'* about that today. We got enough to worry about without you tellin' 'bout the Barksdales and goin' over all that old mess."

Miss Kate turned and ascended the front stairway to her bedroom where she closed the door. She went over to the windowsill and reached behind the curtain and picked up a jelly glass full of whiskey and took a swallow.

"That damned Emma," she muttered out loud, shaking her head. "You can't live with 'em, and you can't live without 'em."

Emma was born at Bright Leaf in 1924, the daughter of Lucy, whose father was Little Zeke. His father was Black Zeke, who was 25 when the War ended in 1865. It was unclear where Black Zeke came from, but he was said to be a giant of a man without a hint of white blood in his veins.

These were the facts, according to the back pages of the leather-bound account book that Big Buck Sims started keeping at about the time the War got serious. He realized he could very well not come home after the War, and he wanted to leave a record of various events and people who were integral to the running of Bright Leaf. The slaves were enumerated along with the livestock, but with the special distinction of an identifying name and age. It was in precisely this fashion that the good horses were also listed.

Kate Sims was four years old when Emma was born in one of the cabins at Bright Leaf. By then, the Negroes were paid weekly wages, but still their dependence upon the Sims family was nearly as great as ever. Emma's mother, Lucy, was the Sims's cook, and from the time Emma was three or four years old, she went to the big house with her mother. Neither Miss Kate nor Emma could recall life without the other, not that either gave it much thought.

Kate Sims had been married three times. Whether by foresight, or just natural instinct, she had never changed her name on any of her bank accounts or business records. She was the same Katherine Wooding Sims that she was the day she was born. She had married twice by the time her beloved father died when she was thirty, but he had lived long enough to teach her never to completely trust anyone—especially Negroes, husbands and grown children. She now knew how right he was about husbands and children, but she had not yet come to a conclusion on Negroes. As for her most recent husband, she got the last laugh on him by burying him alongside the strumpet he died with when the karaoke bar at Myrtle Beach where the girl worked burned up with them both in it.

On this hot summer day, Kate Sims was unhappy that Bobby Barksdale was coming to talk about financial planning, as he called it. The thought alone of the Barksdale Family was enough to send her once more to the jelly glass on the windowsill. And the fresh swallow of whiskey set her to remembering the famous tale Emma liked to tell about Bobby Barksdale's great grandfather, Littleberry Barksdale.

In 1934, when Emma was about ten years old, she was sent over to the Barksdale place, a few miles away, to help out with a family gathering. More than a hundred Barksdales and assorted in-laws had congregated on a beautiful summer Sunday to pray and feast and rejoice over being Barksdales. Dinner was served on the grounds. In his eighty-fifth year, Littleberry Barksdale, the grand patriarch who had narrowly missed serving in the War, presided over the festivities, including offering up the main prayer.

After dinner, the old man went out and took a comfortable chair by himself on his front porch. He called for a second slice of brown sugar pie. It happened that little Emma, who was collecting dinner dishes from the grounds, answered his call and fetched the pie for him from the kitchen. A few minutes later, when Littleberry Barksdale had finished his pie, he summoned Emma again and asked her to go get him a tall glass of cool water. They were his precise words, as Emma always pointed out when she told the story: *A tall glass of cool water.*

Just as Emma started into the house for the water, Littleberry Barksdale abruptly got up and walked directly out to the water well in the side yard. It was a handsome, hand-dug well—wide-throated and about seventy-five feet deep, the source of some of the coolest, nicest water around. Without a moment's hesitation, Littleberry pitched himself over the wooden well box and plunged headfirst to the bottom of the well.

Little Emma could hardly believe what she had seen. She went tearing into the house, screaming that Mister Littleberry had jumped into the well. Of course, no one believed her until they finally went out and looked. There at the bottom, feet skyward, was the Barksdale family patriarch. To Kate Sims, what happened next said something important to her about the Barksdales: The entire family assembled and filed past, each one taking a long look down into the well at what could be seen of old Littleberry. Even the children were held up for a last look and warned about the dangers of fooling around wells, especially diving headfirst into one.

The one person who did not look was Emma, who fled on foot all the way back to Bright Leaf where she immediately assumed her position as the presiding authority on this pivotal event in local history. No one on earth knew more than Emma about the last moments of Littleberry Barksdale. Now, sixty-five years later, Emma still sought any occasion to tell about what she saw at the last major Barksdale reunion.

There's just something peculiar about all those Barksdales, Miss Kate thought, looking out at the old road running through the fields. *It's something that comes down through the blood.* Her own suspicion was that Littleberry was drunk, but the family insisted this was not the case. They pointed out that he had been dried out at a reputable Richmond sanitarium just a few weeks before the reunion. *Too bad a few more of them didn't jump in the well that same day,* she thought.

Then Miss Kate went in to bathe and get ready to receive Bobby Barksdale, whom she found to be one of the most worrisome of all Littleberry's descendants.

Truth was, Kate Sims probably could use some help with her money. While she had plenty of it, thanks to her three husbands and the Bright Leaf tobacco leases, the prospect of leaving her money to her children was a thorny one. All fathered by her second husband, there were three of them—two boys and a purple-haired girl in California named Sally. Sally had married several times and reproduced with impressive regularity. Her unions were so bountiful that Miss Kate could hardly keep the number of children straight—much less their last names and ages. She was a sweet-natured girl who telephoned her mother often and, unlike her brothers, never asked to borrow money. Miss Kate felt warmth for Sally, but she was certain the girl would be a poor choice for handling the Sims land and money. Some man would surely get it.

As for the sons, Jack and Carter, they had settled in New York City where they claimed great success in fields far beyond their mother's comprehension. Carter called himself a creative design consultant in the computer industry. Jack had something to do with trading foreign currencies for a bank. Jack had a bony, mousy little wife named Monique, and two mousy little children, all of whom were brought to Bright Leaf once a year--clearly against their will.

As for Carter, he had never taken to women, leading Emma once to confide to Miss Kate: "I do believe that Mister Carter, he just don't care for girls."

"I 'spect it's worse than that," Kate Sims had replied.

"Yassum," Emma had said.

But Carter and Jack were keenly interested in their mother's finances, with a particular concern over what they called diversifying her assets. As for tax concerns, the prime solution in their view was for Miss Kate to give them most everything she had before she died. As for the thousand acres of land remaining in Bright Leaf, or even the house itself, she did not believe any one of the three had a serious interest in keeping it or ever living in Southside Virginia.

While she would never confide anything important to the likes of Bobby Barksdale, Kate was always curious about what anyone in his business might recommend. Her father had taught her that wisdom lay in listening, especially when it was free. Bobby Barksdale worked for the bank at Shaw's Pond where she had done some of her banking for decades, as had her father and grandfather. In her estimation, the bank had gone down since a big Richmond bank bought it. A good example of this decline, she felt, was the hiring of Bobby Barksdale as a manager.

Now bathed and dressed, Miss Kate reached behind the window curtain for a swallow and then went out into the upstairs hallway where, to her surprise, Emma was waiting.

"Now Emma, when Mister Barksdale gets here, I want you to sit him down in the hall in the green chair, and then I'll come down and take him into the living room. You hear?"

"Yassum."

"And don't say anything about that snake in the parlor, and don't get to talkin' about his great granddaddy jumpin' in the well, awright?"

"Yassum."

"Then you come in a little bit later and ask if you can serve us something, and then you bring him a Coca-Cola. Just bring me some ice water. You understand?"

"Yassum."

"Now, have you looked to see what that snake's doin'?"

"Yassum, I looked in there, and he sound asleep. Don't look like he even moved. You know how nice and cool and quiet it is in that parlor, and you know, Miss Kate, that's what a big old snake what just ate likes…"

"*Emma!* Stop it! I don't want to hear you takin' up for that snake, makin' out like how smart he is. He ain't nothin' but a goddamn snake. I don't want to hear anymore about how he found a nice cool parlor to sleep in. Now how come you upstairs anyway?"

"What I come up here to tell you was that Mister Barksdale, he called on the telephone while you was bathin'? Said he was bringin' a lady with him from the main office, if that was awright with you? I told him you'd be real glad to see her."

"I don't know about that," Miss Kate said. "But if she's comin', she's comin'."

"You want me to serve her a Coca-Cola, too?"

"Yes, Emma, but I don't want to hear a *word* about that snake, you hear now? I don't want that Barksdale boy going back to Shaw's Pond an' tellin' everybody I got a snake layin' on my mantelpiece, you hear!"

"Yassum, but they say that boy's right smart. He might know a good man to work on this snake situration. You just don't never know," Emma said.

"Well, you leave it alone, now you *hear?*" She glared at Emma.

"Yassum."

Upstairs, the two women looked out over the front balcony at the long road where Bobby Barksdale and the lady from the main office would come driving up. Both slightly stooped, Emma's eyes squinting into the outside light, neither gave a moment's thought to the hundreds of times women—young and old, fearful and joyous, downtrodden and angry—had stood watch on that spot for the first sign of an arrival. For the two-hundred years Bright Leaf had stood here, this was the watching spot for the first edition of whatever news was on the way.

"Here he come now!" Emma said brightly. "You can see the dust kickin' up over the hill."

Robert Barksdale, assistant vice-president, was sporting a fresh haircut and an olive summer suit. His crisp shirt was white, his tie striped, his shoes shining. As manager of the Shaw's Pond office of Watchovia Bank, he had been assigned to identify local customers believed to have assets of at least one million dollars. He was then to arrange meetings between those customers and Watchovia's trust department in Richmond with an eye toward creating new trust accounts. He was at the wheel of a prudent little gray sedan the bank provided for visits like this one.

Next to Robert Barksdale sat Alexandra Cobbett, a small woman with dark eyes and blonde hair wrapped tightly around her head. Called Allie, she was an associate trust officer of the Watchovia trust department in Richmond, which had launched an aggressive campaign for business under the slogan: *At Watchovia, We Watch Over You.* Allie Cobbett wore a dark skirt and white blouse. A deep blue and red silk scarf was draped over her neck and fell from a loosely tied knot. Even in the sunlight, her skin seemed lustrous. She had grown up in California and come east for her early banking experience.

"Like I was tellin' you, Miss Kate's kind of a mess," young Barksdale said, giggling faintly. "Just don't let her get to you, Allie. She don't mean anything by what she says, she just has her own way, you know what I mean? But I know she's got *plenty* of money she needs help with." Bobby slid a grin toward Allie.

"That's why we're going to see her, Bobby. Remember?" Allie Cobbett seemed in a dark humor and had snapped at him several times that morning as he sought to advise her about local people and customs.

Bitch, Bobby thought. "Well, yeah, Allie, I know that, but I'm just tellin' you, like I say, Miss Kate's a mess and sometime she can just get all over you, and I tell you, she didn't sound all that happy we're comin'. All I'm sayin' is for you not to let her get under your skin, you know? She can worry you to death if you let her. You know what I mean?"

"Bobby, you make it very clear what you mean, and I thank you," said Allie. "If she's got money, and if she'll trust us with some of it, then we can help her. It's not complicated." Allie riffled through some papers in her lap. Her tanned fingers, nails neatly manicured, were long and graceful. Her only jewelry was a small gold watch on her left wrist, and small gold earrings. "How much did you tell me we think her estate's worth?"

"No way to know for sure. She banks all over the place, even in New York City. She's got around two hundred and fifty with Watchovia, mainly in certificates. We figure she got a lot of money out of her husbands, she's had three of them, and she hit 'em all pretty good, and she's got about the biggest tobacco farm left around here."

"It's hard to believe nobody is giving her estate advice," Allie said. "How do you know she doesn't have a trust relationship with one of the banks away from here?"

"What can I say?" Barksdale shuffled his shoulders. "I guess I don't know. I do know she hires a lot of lawyers. She loves to sue people and cause trouble. She's just a mess."

"So, we really have no idea whether she has a trust relationship with another bank, do we?" Allie said.

Bitch, Barksdale thought. "I just cain't say one way or the other," he said. "We'll just have to sort of feel her out." Allie Cobbett sighed as they got closer and parked by the tall boxwood at the side of the house. Barksdale straightened his tie, shot his cuffs and checked his image in the car's mirror before getting out. He saw Allie roll her eyes as she got out. Then she spoke to him over the top of the car: "You look beautiful, Bobby," she said, without a trace of a smile.

Bitch. "And so do you," he said. "But it won't mean squat to Miss Kate what either of us look like. Like I told you, she's a mess, a real mess, and if she's hungry, she'll eat us both alive."

They walked along a flagstone path beneath giant Black Walnut trees to the front of the house. Bobby's leather shoe soles clicked brightly on the stone steps as he strode up and gave the heavy iron knocker two polite raps.

When the door opened, short, broad-bottomed Emma stood waiting in a loose-fitting blue serving dress and a stiff white apron. "Why you come on in, Mister Bobby," she said, taking his hand. "Now ain't it good to see you, and I reckon this is the nice lady from the main office you said you was bringin'?"

"Yes, Emma, this is Miss Cobbett...."

"Allie's my name, Emma," she said, smiling and taking Emma's hand. "I'm glad to see you."

"Hot, ain't it," Emma said. "Y'all come in now, and let's get this door shut and try to keep the cool in and this heat out. Have to do a lot of that on a good old hot summer day like this, now don't we, Mister Bobby?"

"You bet we do," Barksdale said. "Yessir, we have to keep the cool in and the heat out. That's what we do down South, now idn't that right, Emma?"

"Yessir, now Mister Bobby, you sit here in the green chair, and Miss, why don't you sit right over here in this white chair, and I'll go up and tell Miss Kate y'all is here to see her, and of course you know she's lookin' for you."

Emma started slowly down the hall to the back staircase.

Bobby sat down in the green chair at once, but Allie began wandering about the center hall looking at the paintings and family portraits.

"You better sit down!" Bobby said to Allie. "Miss Kate's right particular about who sits where."

"Oh, *please!*" Allie said, continuing her inspection.

A few minutes later, they heard a little rustle at the top of the staircase, and Kate Sims began her descent, a surprisingly quick-paced gait considering her eighty-five years. She wore a floral-patterned silk blouse and a white linen skirt, set off with a Goliath-sized diamond brooch. Her grayish blonde hair was swept back, her gray eyes a little hooded. The Sims lip relaxed into a gentle smile as she cleared the last step and assumed command.

"Why, it's *wonderful* of you all to come out on such a hot old day. We see so few people down here anymore, being so far out and everything, and now it's gotten to where in the summer we look like Little Mexico around here, with all these Mexicans doin' the work our own people won't do anymore."

As Bobby rose respectfully, Allie moved quickly to Miss Kate. "Miz Sims, thank you for letting us come. I'm Allie Cobbett, and what a beautiful home you have! I *love* the name Bright Leaf."

"Why thank you. It's just home to us, always has been, hope it always will be," Kate Sims said, warmly.

"Are those *English* boxwood out there?" Allie said. "I think I've never seen any so big and healthy."

"Oh yes," Miss Kate said. "We have to take care of our box. It's older than any of us, heard more secrets told out there than the man in the moon. Good thing they don't talk. Probably heard Momma and Poppa courting." Miss Kate held the young woman's hand in both of hers. "Now, Miss... Tell me your name again?"

"Please call me Allie," she said. "I'll give you a card, but Allie Cobbett is my name." Just then, a faintly familiar smell scooted by Allie's nose. *Whiskey?* she wondered. *Not at midday,* she told herself, and dismissed the thought.

"And how are *you*, Bobby Barksdale," Miss Kate said, moving toward him. "It's always nice to see you. Been knowin' you since before you were house-broke, but we won't talk about that, now will we?"

Barksdale giggled. "Why Miss Kate, I just been tellin' Allie how much you always meant to me and my family..."

"Come on, now Bobby," Miss Kate said. "I can't imagine what you'd be sayin' about me to this lady. Do tell, I'd love to hear it."

Allie laughed out loud, a throaty, real laugh from down deep.

"Aw, now, Miss Kate," Barksdale said, attempting to chuckle instead of giggle. "You just joshin' me. I know you."

"Well, let's just both *not* tell what we been sayin' about each other," Miss Kate said. She laughed a merry laugh. "Y'all come on, and we'll sit in the livin' room and have a nice little visit." She started that way.

"Why, Miss Kate," said Barksdale, following her. "Many times as I've been here, I don't think I've ever been in the livin' room, 'less it was for a funeral or something. Seems like we always sit in the parlor. And when I was little, I *loved* to sit in your parlor and we'd look at all the little curiosities on the mantel, like that little music box, and the watches, and all sorts of nice little curiosities...."

Emma had just entered the room to see what people wanted to drink and heard the comment. "Lord!" she said suddenly. "You oughta see the curiosity we got on that mantel today!"

"*Emma*, what in the world is the matter with you!" said Miss Kate sharply. "Somebody'd think you have a brain tumor, talkin' like that. Bobby, that mantel is just like it always was. We're just waitin' to have some work done in there, so I thought it would be nice to sit in here. *If that's awright with Emma!*" Miss Kate glowered at the little black woman.

"Yassum, Miss Kate," said Emma, chastened. "Now what I come in for was to say I'd like to bring y'all sumpin' cool to drink on a hot day like this? We got some Coca-Colas nice and cold?"

"Yes," said Allie, "That would be just right for me, thank you."

As Emma turned to Miss Kate and Bobby Barksdale, Allie got up and walked over to look at a framed lithographic print on the wall by the door. "This is an Edward Beyer, isn't it?" she said.

"Why yes," Miss Kate said, clearly pleased. "So you know his work?"

"Not all that well, but this is handsome. Looks like it came right out of the book."

"Yes, I'm sorry to say, it probably did," Miss Kate said. "Don't you think it's terrible how they tear up books and frame the pages? I know I hate it, but when I saw that print down in Charleston, I just had to have it. One of my great grandmothers came from Augusta County, and her homeplace there looked so much like that one. I love havin' it, but I know somebody probably tore up the book for the prints."

"Oh no, Miss Kate," said Allie, sensing Barksdale catching his breath. "That's not the way to look at it. What probably happened is that the book got nearly destroyed by a flood or a fire or something, and just a few pages were saved, and now this one is preserved and hanging here in a lovely room where people can appreciate it."

"Well, that's a nice way to look at it, but I don't know how appreciated it is," Miss Kate said. "In the thirty years it's been here, you're the first person who ever knew what it was or even asked about it." She cut her eyes at Barksdale.

Emma had returned with the cool drinks. Miss Kate eyed Allie. She admired the girl's polished features and general poise, her way of saying thank-you with a slight tip of her head. "You sure are a pretty girl," Miss Kate said. "I don't believe you from around here, now, are you?"

"My family is from Virginia, actually from right here in William Byrd County, but I grew up in California," Allie said. "The only reason I know about Edward Beyer is that my grandmother in Richmond has one of his prints of a scene in Montgomery County. That's where her family came from."

"Who knows?" Miss Kate said. "Could of come out of the same book." Then, startled, she added, "You say you grew up in *California*? My daughter Sally's been out there for years, and she sure didn't look like you."

"Oh?" Allie said. "What does she do in California?"

"To start with, Sally has purple hair, or did the last time I saw her, she did. I thought maybe a lot of people out there had purple hair. Can you imagine makin' your hair purple!"

"That's interesting," Allie said. "Actually, I don't think I know anyone with purple hair. Maybe Sally has started something."

"Well, whatever she's doin' out there's a puzzle to me, but she's a sweet girl," Miss Kate said, turning toward the center hall. "Y'all gonna have to excuse me for just a minute, I need to get some papers I left in the parlor." As she got up and started easing out of the room, Bobby Barksdale, whose head had been bobbing between the two women, jumped to his feet, smiling broadly.

"That's good, Miss Kate. Go get those papers. We need to get down to business." Ignoring Bobby, she silently passed out of the room.

A moment later, Emma appeared with a silver tray, asking if she could bring them anything else. "Lordy mercy, Emma!" Barksdale said, suddenly energized and jovial with Kate Sims safely out of the room. "Just don't bring us *another slice of brown sugar pie* or a *tall glass of cool water!*" He clapped his hands and hooted with laughter. "Allie, don't look so puzzled. That's just a little family thing between me and Emma, now idn't that right Emma?"

"Well, since you bring it up, and I'm awready in trouble with Miss Kate about talkin' about our parlor, but that business you talkin' about with the *brown sugar pie* and the *tall glass of cool water*, now that was a mess, now won't it? Your daddy, he was there that day, just a baby, but he was one the ones they carried to look down the well…"

"What was in the well?" Allie said.

"Nothin', Miss," Emma said. "But I tell you, that Miss Kate, she gets awful put out when I go to tellin' about it."

Beaming, Barksdale reassured Allie, "Now don't you worry about it, this is just family stuff," he said. "Neither here nor there, as they say on TeeVee."

"Well, I'm *here* and you're *there!*" Kate Sims said fiercely as she stood in the doorway, having just returned from the parlor. "I heard everything y'all talkin' about, and Bobby Barksdale, why in the world would you bring up all your family mess in front of this nice pretty girl? You oughta be tryin' to make a good showin' with her, not haulin' skeletons out your closet."

"Well," Barksdale said. "Emma, she, uh, you know how she always brings it up…"

"She didn't bring it up this time!" Miss Kate said. "I'd just come out of the parlor and heard *you* bring it up!"

"Lord, Miss Kate," Emma said. "You mean you been back in that parlor? You told me we won't goana say a word about what's in that parlor."

"We're *not*, Emma! I had to go in there and straighten the drapes and get some business papers, which I still seem to have left in there." Miss Kate put her hands out in a mildly helpless gesture.

"Aaaah, that mysterious parlor again," Allie said. "And what on earth was in that well…I seem to be the only one who doesn't know." Allie's nostrils twitched faintly as a little ghost of whiskey hovered nearby for a moment, just like when she arrived.

"Well," Miss Kate said. "I certainly don't care if you know, since Bobby Barksdale brought the whole thing up. I don't know why anyone would bring up sumpin' so sorry about his own family, like he's braggin' about it or sumpin'. They oughta all be ashamed of it."

"Well, Miss Kate, if you want to talk about it," Barksdale said, "Emma can tell the whole story, since she was the only witness and is still the main expert..."

"No sir," Miss Kate said. "I'm tired, *real* tired, of hearin' Emma tell that story. I've been listenin' to her tell it all my damn life, and that's enough. If it's goana be told this afternoon, Bobby Barksdale, I want to hear *you* tell it!"

"But Miss Kate, I know you just tryin' to josh me. You know I won't there when it happened. But I can tell you this. Until the day he died, my daddy, he claimed he could remember his daddy holding him up so he could see down in the well..."

"...What was in the well!" Allie said.

"...And that's exactly why I think all you Barksdales are so curious," Miss Kate pressed on, "cause all of you looked down the well and took a big spell from it that lasts 'til this day!"

Allie got up, looking annoyed, and began making her way around the room, studying the pictures on the walls and the odds and ends on the tables. She occasionally brushed an object with her fingertip, as if to test it to some standard known only to her. With Barksdale and Miss Kate yammering about who would tell the story about Littleberry Barksdale jumping down the well, Emma sidled up to Allie and spoke in a low voice.

"Now, Miss, you just make yourself at home, but be sure you don't go in the parlor. We got some things going on in there we need to tend to, some right big things, well, *one* big thing, but Miss Kate, she ain't wantin' nobody in that parlor because, you know, Mister Bobby, he talk so much..."

"Emma, what's in the parlor? A dead body?"

"No ma'am, it ain't dead, and that's the main trouble, but I can't say no more." Emma eased away.

Allie made her way over to one of the front windows of the living room and stood looking down the long road. On either side were rows and rows of heavy green tobacco, stretching over gentle hills to the woods in the distance. She could see the brown-skinned men working quickly along the rows. Off to her left, she could see where the Nolting River ran along the boundary of the property. She could see the graveyard.

As she stood there at the window, Allie again sensed the little ghost of whiskey that kept flitting around the room. Her nose twitched. Then her eyes fell on a jelly glass sitting on the windowsill behind the drape. Gently, with one finger, she pulled the drape back and looked down at the amber liquid. *Whiskey,* she realized. *This must be what I keep smelling.*

Emma had left the room, and Allie could hear Miss Kate and Bobby prattling behind her on the other side of the room. She picked up the glass and smelled it—bourbon, she figured. The hot, heavy smell of it almost made her gag. She put the glass down and looked again out the long dirt road running through old Bright Leaf plantation. She looked again at the graveyard, its rock wall still in stately, if mellowed, condition. Her eyes fell on the parade line of fieldstone markers outside the rock wall—each signifying a long forgotten slave who had not had a name worth remembering. Then she thought about what could have been in that Barksdale well they were still jabbering about, and she wondered about what lurked in the parlor across the hall.

Allie Cobbett's family had been in William Byrd County, living at Shaw's Pond, since the town and county were founded. But Allie had never lived there. Her parents had divorced in the wake of her father's decision to move back to Shaw's Pond to run the family's newspaper. Allie's mother, an educated Richmond woman of good intelligence, believed with all her heart and soul that the very soil and water of Shaw's Pond was no good for the Cobbett children. She would not consent to seeing her children grow up there.

Thus, when Allie's father, Sam Cobbett, went home to Shaw's Pond to run the newspaper, her mother took Allie and her brother, Little Sam, to California and started a new life. Several years had passed since Allie had had any contact with her father. The emotional divide was such that she thought it was too complicated to get in touch with him on this current business trip to Shaw's Pond and William Byrd County.

As Allie stood at the window, looking down the road, something powerful came over her, as though she had become for a moment a part of something she had never known, something with a primal tug on her spirit.

Her mother had never really explained why she had such strong feelings against living at Shaw's Pond, beyond sniping that most of the people were crazy and obsessed with the past. Allie picked up the jelly glass and took a full, deep drink of the straight whiskey. Her eyes squinted and she muffled a gasp and a small gag. Then she felt a sort of music in the form of a warm tingle dancing across her shoulders. She put the jelly glass back behind the drape.

What a nice place to be, she thought, cozily, staring across the tobacco fields.

Allie Cobbett's reverie was broken when she realized Emma was at her side, speaking in a hushed tone. "Miss Kate, she told me to come get you, she needs you to do sumpin', but she don't want Mister Bobby to know nothin' about it."

"Where's Bobby?" Allie said, looking around.

"Miss Kate, she done sent him down to the cellar, with the big ring of old keys that don't fit nothin'? You know, and told him to figure out which key unlocks the old store room down there? She say her bidness papers down there. Told him not to come back 'til he figured out which key works."

"What does Bobby know about opening locks?" Allie said.

"He don't know nothin'," Emma said. "That's why she sent him down there, keep him busy and out the way. Miss Kate, she gets tired real quick of them Barksdales..."

"Yes, I've gathered that," Allie said. "They all looked down in the water well, right?"

"Yassum, that's right. Miss Kate thinks that's why they all so curious, but me, I know they was curious a long time before all that stuff happened."

"So, Bobby's in the cellar. Where's Miss Kate?"

"She in the parlor, and she told me to come get you, but she don't want you to say nothin' about what you might see in the parlor, but she say she thinks you might have some idea about how to handle our situration in there..."

"Well, Emma, first you have got to tell me what *was* in the bottom of the well?"

"It were Mister Littleberry," Emma said solemnly.

"Oh," Allie said. "I see. And he was a Barksdale?"

"Yassum, he was the main Barksdale, and I was there and I was the last person talked to him when he ask for a second slice of brown sugar pie and a tall glass of cool water, and I was the only person to see him climb up and jump head-first down the well…"

"Good lord, Emma, I want to hear all about it sometime, but right now, is Miss Kate waiting for me in the parlor?"

"Yassum, and I'll open the door real quiet for you, and you keep your voice low so we don't make no noise."

"*Emma!* Where you? *Emma!*" Miss Kate was in the center hall calling.

"Yassum, I'm comin'," Emma said, bustling away, leaving Allie standing there by the window. "Now you come on along real quick," Emma called over her shoulder. With hardly a thought, Allie reached behind the drape for the jelly glass and took another deep swallow of the whiskey, willing her stomach to accept the harsh assault. Another nice tingle danced across her shoulders.

"I'll be right there," she called after Emma.

Miss Kate stood in the center hall, brows furrowed, the Sims lip in full pout. She seemed to be glowering at Allie, who said, "Miss Kate, are you okay?"

"No I'm not," she said. "We got a problem in the parlor. A right big one, and I'm startin' to get mad about it. We were fixin' to send for this Catholic shoe cobbler, Mister Karewski, over at Bog Town, but Emma thinks he's dead. I'd just like to get this thing settled without involvin' too many people, and I can tell you a smart girl, and I thought you might have some ideas."

"Yassum," Allie Cobbett said.

"Don't you *yassum* me, young lady!" Miss Kate's glower deepened and the Sims lip poked out even further. "Don't nobody but Emma *YASSUM* me!"

"I'm so sorry, Miss Kate," Allie said, bewildered. "I didn't mean to say that, I really didn't. It just came out. It's something about being here in this nice setting…I don't know, I can't explain it, but I'm sorry and I won't say it again."

"You're a real pretty girl when you get off balance a little bit, now aren't you?" Miss Kate was smiling now, and her voice had gone to a little-girl high, almost a pitty-pat baby talk. "I bet you even prettier when you get mad." Allie's young, unlined face showed the crinkle of a little dimple next to her mouth.

"Thank you, Miss Kate." Allie said. "Don't you think we'd better talk about the estate planning we came to discuss with you?"

"I'd never think you were from California, no sir-ree-Bob, I wouldn't," Miss Kate said in the high little-girl voice. The whisper of whiskey in the air was now much more pronounced.

"Well, I have a lot of family here in Virginia," Allie said. "Do you know of the Cobbetts at Shaw's Pond?"

"Do I know the Cobbetts! I know 'em all. Know 'em well," Miss Kate said. "Sometimes I like those Cobbetts and sometimes I don't. It just depends on what they put in that damn newspaper of theirs."

"That paper has caused a lot of trouble in my family, for a long time," Allie said. "I guess you know my dad, Sam Cobbett? He came back here to run it."

"Good God, I know all the Sam Cobbetts. The one's there now is your daddy? Good gracious! I was sweet, real sweet, on the one I guess would be your great grandfather, a wonderful man, the sort of man I liked to talk to, but I could always tell he was a little standoffish toward me."

"I remember him when I was a little girl, when we'd come from Washington for quick visits, but I never really knew him, but my dad was crazy about him."

"But I don't understand about you and your daddy," Miss Kate said. "He was good friends with my son Jack and used to come down here visiting a lot. Real nice boy. I haven't seen him in ages." She was impatient now, glancing toward the parlor.

"I don't understand all of it," Allie said. "My mom just said she would divorce him if he went through with moving back here to run the paper. And she did. It was as if she thought there was something in the air and water around here that could take over your spirit and soul and just keep them and lock them up forever. I wish I understood it better. I mean, whatever this is, California isn't the best place to grow up either."

"You said you live in Richmond now and work at the bank, but right now, are you staying with your daddy at Shaw's Pond?"

"No ma'am," Allie said, becoming uncomfortable for the first time. "He doesn't even know I'm here. We just don't keep up. I haven't talked to him since I was in college, and he was paying for some of it."

"Well, I can talk all day and all night about the Cobbetts, and I can tell it any way you wanta hear it." Miss Kate said. "One thing about 'em though, is that they're smart people, not like these damn hopeless Barksdales."

"I just don't know much about things around here," Allie said. "Sometimes I wish I did. I always thought Shaw's Pond was a beautiful little town to look at."

"Well, I can tell you one thing," Miss Kate said, her voice going soft, the Sims lip receding. "That Shaw's Pond *is* a pretty little town, except for the damned *people*."

"Well, I just don't know," Allie said. "But Miss Kate, let's go sit down and talk about estate planning. It's something we all need to do…"

"Estate plannin'?" Miss Kate said, incredulous. "What is there to plan? What do I care about what happens when I'm dead and gone? It's a big waste of time, especially when I got a real problem right here in the parlor, and I'm talkin' about the sort of problem we need somebody to fix right now, not after we're dead and gone."

"Well, tell me," Allie said.

"I better just show you," Miss Kate said. "But you need to be quiet as midnight when we go in there, 'cause we don't want to stir him up."

"It's not Littleberry Barksdale, is it?"

"*What?*" Miss Kate said sharply. "Of course not. That was a problem, awright, but it got solved when the old fool jumped in that well."

Miss Kate eased the parlor door open and then turned and, in a whisper, told Emma to remain in the center hall, adding: "If that Bobby Barksdale comes up here whinin' about how none of the keys fit, you send him right back down there and tell him I said for him to keep tryin'. Tell him he needs to learn persistence," she added.

"Yassum," Emma said.

They slipped into the darkened parlor. It took a moment for Allie's eyes to adjust, but then she made it out. It was less formal than the living room and seemed to have nice books and a wealth of family-related objects.

"Now our problem," Miss Kate whispered, "is over yonder draped across the mantel. Can you see what I'm looking at?"

"Yes, I see it," Allie said. "Looks like a snake to me. Is it stuffed?"

"Oh no, no!" Miss Kate said. "That's the trouble, you see. He's alive. He's all laid up there wound around all our nice little things, like my daddy's gold watch in that bell jar, and my granddaddy's buttons from his uniform, and see that jeweled music box with the crystal dancer on top? Why, that music box, it's been involved in two great big lawsuits. It came from Tiffany's up in New York City, and they say it's worth fifty thousand dollars for the jewels alone. It's a pretty thing, used to play the Bright Leaf Waltz, but it hadn't chirped a peep in years. Somebody wound it too tight, or somethin'."

"How did the snake get up there?" Allie said.

"We just don't know. I do know a snake's a tricky thing. He probably came down the chimley and worked his way around. I've seen 'em go right up the side of a buildin' where you wouldn't think they had a thing to hang onto, and Lord knows they whip through tall trees like monkeys when they get to feastin' on the little new birds. And last summer, out in the side yard, Emma was after one with our hoe, and he went like a shot cat right into a downspout and went all the way up and come out on the roof! I mean to tell you, a snake is a tricky thing."

"So, what are you going to do about this one?" Allie said.

"Emma wanted to go after him with our hoe, you know, cut off his tail up around his ears, and our hoe is real sharp, but if we did that, he'd get to fightin' and carryin' on and no tellin' what he'd bust up. Those nice little things would just smash on the hearth. How come you not bothered by this snake? Lot of people have a fit."

"I don't know enough for them to bother me," Allie said. "But I don't see why it would be hard to get him down, if nobody gets excited."

"And that's why I don't want them Mexicans comin' in here and tryin' to move him out of here. They get all excited and talk funny and no telling what that old snake would do listening to all that."

"I understand," Allie said. "So why don't you let me work on it."

"Now that's just what I had in mind," Miss Kate said. "I could tell you're a smart girl and that you would see this thing in clear light. And I know you won't be goin' back to Shaw's Pond and tellin' everybody all up and down the street about our predicament. If that damn fool Bobby Barksdale thinks it's funny about his great granddaddy jumpin' in that well, he'd probably think this situation was funny, too, and then he'd go back and tell folks I'm down here at Bright Leaf keepin' company with a big old snake in my parlor. Make people think there's sumpin' wrong with us down here."

"Well, I don't know, Miss Kate. I really don't know Bobby very well..."

"That speaks well for you," Miss Kate said. "You should keep it that way, but what do you think we can do about this snake?"

"Tell you what," Allie said. "If you want me to try, then I need to think about this by myself. Now don't take this the wrong way, but how about you going across the hall and sitting down in the living room and leaving me right here by myself to see if I can figure out something?"

When Miss Kate had gone, Allie went directly over to the windowsill and found a jelly glass behind the drape. Only an inch of whiskey was left. She quaffed it and sat down in the chair and looked out the window. From across the hall in the living room, Allie heard Miss Kate yelling for Emma. Allie had no doubt that Miss Kate was summoning Emma to explain why the jelly glass behind the living room drape that should have been full was nearly empty. Allie's smile turned to giggles—soft giggles, just to herself. *So this must be part of why my mom was so determined not to let us live here,* she thought. *It's like a world I never knew existed, and at any moment the Mad Hatter could come along.*

After a few minutes, Allie slipped silently across the room and stood at the tail end of the snake. She ran her finger across the mantel's wood surface, just behind the snake. The soot on her fingertip confirmed that he probably had arrived through the chimney.

At least a dozen items of varying size stood along the mantel. Some were delicate crystal and glass figurines, as well as the objects Miss Kate had mentioned. Indeed, it was hard to fathom how the snake had managed to get into the present position without knocking over anything. It was even harder to imagine how he might be successfully removed.

The only item the snake's body was actually resting on was a corner of the Tiffany music box—the item Miss Kate had said was worth fifty thousand dollars. Otherwise, the items were fractions of an inch away from the snake's body, no more than an inch here and an inch there.

Starting at the tail end, Allie began removing each item the snake was not touching. She carefully placed each little treasure on an empty bookshelf nearby. Working quietly and quickly, she had removed most of the items when the snake barely moved, just a twitch. She froze. But that was its only movement.

Now, the one thing left was the Tiffany music box upon which a bit of the serpent's body rested. Allie moved her face close to examine just how much of the snake was on the music box. The smell of the snake filled her nostrils, a deep musty odor with an aliveness to it. She had resisted touching the snake, but now she gently pressed the tip of one finger to its skin. It was firm and smooth, even velvety, like a giant elongated muscle. There was no reaction from the serpent.

Allie studied the features of the little dancer atop the music box. Tiny rubies and green garnets and other jewels were dotted in the dancer's dress. Little diamonds decorated a tiara. The dancer stood on one leg, in a pirouette. Allie could see that the figure was made to twirl when the music box was activated. She saw the tiny release switch on the music box and remembered that Miss Kate had explained that it had been wound too tight years earlier and would not play. Allie's long finger gently jiggled the release switch. Instantly, there was music, a brisk tinkling waltz. And then motion. As the dancer began to twirl, a glass hand scraped across the serpent's body.

Startled by this, Allie stood back and tried to recognize the familiar waltz. Then, ever so slowly, almost fluidly, the serpent began to move. When Allie looked to her left, she saw the snake's head and six inches of its body hanging forward from the mantel's edge, wavering gracefully. Then it found the wall and moved downward to the top of the chair rail and then along the wainscoting and soon the front of the snake was on the floor. The rest of the snake glided over the edge, never slipping. Once down to the floor, the serpent slithered toward motionless Allie, tongue darting, and veered slowly and surely to its left and into the fireplace. She saw its head rise again, seeming to sense its way, and then slowly disappear into the darkness of the fireplace, moving over the andirons and upwards, until the tip of its tail vanished.

The music box had fallen silent. But when Allie thumped it gently, it came alive, the sparkling dancer twirling to an energetic little waltz. She smiled and shook her head in wonder, relishing her little whiskey buzz. She thought of her mother's admonitions about Shaw's Pond, recalling that she always said it was just too complicated to explain why she did not want her children to grow up here. Was this remarkable and seductive visit to Bright Leaf a taste of what concerned her mother?

Allie looked at the soot on the mantel and then looked around for something she could use to clean it off. She could find nothing. She settled on her silk scarf. She untied it and wiped up all the soot, and then stashed the scarf under the cushions of the sofa, deep down by the springs. Then she put all the little items back at their appointed places on the mantelpiece.

At 23, Allie Cobbett had always been credited with good, if unusual, instincts. It did not occur to her to rush out and explain how she got the snake off the mantelpiece—or how come the music box was now working. It came naturally to her to realize that she was now in possession of some things of great significance to Miss Kate Sims. Allie went into the center hall.

"Miss Kate," she called. "Miss Kate?"

"Do I hear music?" Kate Sims said as she emerged from the living room. "Why, I *do* hear music, dancing music, coming from the parlor!" Her smile was glowing. "When my husband gave me that music box, he said the music was called *The Bright Leaf Waltz*. Said he had it written special. He said that our life here was like a long nice waltz. I used to think it was so sweet of him. How did you fix it?"

"Don't make me tell all my secrets," Allie said, smiling at Miss Kate.

"Do you like the little tune, *The Bright Leaf Waltz*?" Miss Kate asked dreamily. It was clear to Allie that Kate Sims was showing some effects of her visits to the jelly glasses.

"Oh yes," Allie said. "The tone is beautiful, and I think maybe the music has another name in addition to *The Bright Leaf Waltz*, but I can't name it."

"Probably does," Miss Kate said. "That husband was such a goddamned liar. Have you ever been married?"

"No, not even close," Allie said.

"Well don't," Kate Sims said. "It's not worth it. They're all after the same thing, your money and you know what else. You weren't able to do anything about that snake, were you?"

"Truth is, Miss Kate, the snake just didn't like hearing *The Bright Leaf Waltz*. Soon as I got the music going you could tell he was ready to leave. And he did! Just picked his way along and didn't hurt anything."

"Lordy, Chile! Don't tease an old woman like that. I bet that snake hadn't moved and we're still goana have to call somebody to get him out."

For the first time since Allie arrived, Kate Sims seemed a little addled, maybe showing her liquor. "Will you excuse me?" she said. "I need to go in here in the parlor and straighten that drape. I saw it was all pulled around wrong."

"Of course," Allie said, standing aside as Miss Kate entered the parlor. Then there was silence.

"Emma!" Miss Kate called out over the tinkling notes of *The Bright Leaf Waltz*. "Get in here. What happened to the goddamn snake!" Emma rushed past Allie into the parlor.

"Lord have mercy," Emma said softly. "Why, he done arisen and gone, I do believe. He had him that nice nap and rested up in the cool and just went on his way, now ain't that sumpin'?"

"Oh, Emma! *Stop it!* Where's that girl from the bank? *You!* Allie, right? That's right, you're a Cobbett. Come in here. Listen, what did you do with that snake?"

"Miss Kate, I told you he didn't like the music, but maybe we all just think the snake was here.....

"Of course there was a snake on my mantel, and no tellin' what's busted up over there." Miss Kate bustled across to the mantelpiece. She studied the figurines and lightly touched the twirling figure on the Tiffany music box. She could find nothing amiss on the mantel. Then she ran a finger over the wood's surface.

"To get in here, that snake had to come down the chimley, so he had to leave soot," she said. Miss Kate looked at her clean fingertip and then at Allie: "Young lady, what'd you do with him?"

"Nothing, Miss Kate. What would I do with a snake? And why are you so worried about it?" Allie said, a little teasingly. "Isn't this sort of like the old saying that all's well that ends well? No snake is here. Nothing's broken. Nobody knows about it. If we just settle down, everything will be fine. Maybe it was all kind of like in a dream."

"And the music box is fixed," Miss Kate said, looking curiously at Allie. You're a right smart girl, aren't you? You Cobbetts have always been smart." Miss Kate moved over to the window and looked out across the tobacco fields to the graveyard. "I loved Poppa so much," she said quietly. "And I think about him whenever I look over yonder at the graveyard. But then everything about him and Momma and my brothers and sisters and all the coloreds, it all gets real dreamy sometimes. And Poppa, he used to let me lick his spoon every morning. Then sometimes I get to wondering whether it really happened, or whether I sort of dreamed it, and then I get to wondering what difference it makes. If you *think* it happened and you *like* it, isn't that about the same as it really happening?"

"I don't know," Allie said. "You're in too deep for me. Miss Kate, I've gotten awfully thirsty, do you think I could have something to drink?"

"You want ice water or Coca-Cola?" Miss Kate said sharply.

"You don't serve anything stronger, do you? I think a drink of whiskey would be nice."

"No indeed!" Miss Kate said. "Poppa always taught us not to serve anything strong like that. He said it leads to confusion. And sometimes worse."

"Lord," Emma said, "Wouldn't that be sumpin' if we took to *servin'* that stuff around here."

At that moment, the women heard a powerful racket coming from the cellar, and a fast-paced clumping on the steps. Red-faced, his tie askew, Bobby Barksdale burst into the center hall, dropping the big ring of useless keys; they clattered across the floor.

"Lord God almighty!" he bellowed.

"*Look out, Miss Kate!*" Emma screamed. "I can see it comin'. If he can find a well, he's ready to jump!"

"Hush up, Emma!" Miss Kate said. "What's wrong with you, Bobby?"

Breathless, Bobby Barksdale gripped the door frame as he spoke: "I don't know what you gonna do, Miss Kate, but there's the biggest black snake I *ever* seen laid out on that cool soapstone in your basement, and he must of just got there because he sure won't there when I went down."

"I just don't believe it!" Miss Kate said. "Dammit, after all we been through today, to have you come in here with a tale like that...."

"It's God's truth," Bobby Barksdale said, catching his breath. "That snake, he's a huge snake, he's laying all over your basement like somebody spilled black motor oil, and something else I better tell you, he's got a lump in his belly that shows he just ate, and you know how a big old snake loves to eat and then find a nice cool place to rest..."

"Oh, calm down, Bobby," Miss Kate said. Her voice was gentle but impatient. She picked up the ring of keys from the floor and stood fingering them. "Did you try all these keys?" she said.

"Yessum," he said, shaking his head resolutely. "Not a one of the keys fit the storeroom lock. I tried all of 'em over and over. But Miss Kate, listen, I can't go back down there. I just can't stand a great big old snake like that, I mean, what's he goana do after he rests up..."

"Just hush, Bobby," Miss Kate said. "It's probably just a dream dancin' in your head...."

"It's not a dream in *my* head, Miss Kate," he said.

"Allie!" Miss Kate took her by the upper arm and led her toward the cellar door. "Go down there and see what in the world Bobby Barksdale's talkin' about."

"Lord have mercy," Emma muttered as they listened to Allie's footsteps tripping down the stairwell. A few minutes later she returned.

"Nothing down there I saw," Allie said to Miss Kate, with a glint in her eyes.

"I didn't think it would be," Miss Kate said. "But it's high time you took Bobby Barksdale back to Shaw's Pond. He's gotten so nervous and confused that I'm worried he'll have a stroke, or sumpin'."

"I'm ready to go," Bobby said. "But we hadn't talked about estate plannin'."

"And we're not goin' to," Miss Kate said. "Allie, you better drive this boy. These Barksdales just get so nervous I doubt he can drive, and I wouldn't want anything to happen to y'all."

"And don't let him get around any wells," Emma added. Bobby Barksdale was already out the front door when Miss Kate asked for a word with Allie.

"Do you always have Bobby with you when you make these calls?"

"Of course not," Allie said. "He came today because he's such close friends with you."

"Well, truth is, I do have some business things I'd like to talk with you about, but like you might of noticed, I don't have much confidence in Bobby."

"That's fine,"" Allie said. "I'd welcome a chance to discuss anything you like. I'm staying at the hotel in Lynchburg for a couple of days and have some more appointments set up. When would you like for me to come back?"

"How 'bout tomorrow at four o'clock sharp?"

"See you then!" Allie said, smiling and extending her hand. Miss Kate brushed past the hand and gave her a warm little hug.

"And before you go," Miss Kate said, "How 'bout winding up the little music box. Very gently."

Kate Sims and Emma stood at the parlor window watching the two bankers drive away, Allie at the wheel. They were quiet as the *Bright Leaf Waltz* bounced along from the Tiffany music box on the mantelpiece.

"I tell you, Emma, that's a beautiful young girl, smart, too, and she's goana get whatever she wants outa her life," Miss Kate said. "She might not know it yet, but I bet she'll handle it just fine and probably do a lot better'n I did."

"I bet you'd like to be in her shoes, now wouldn't you Miss Kate? You could just start all over again."

"Naw, Emma. Once is enough," Miss Kate said.

"Yassum, now what we goana do 'bout the snake in the basement?"

"The girl said he won't there, but she might of been messin' with us. Whatever, why don't we just leave him alone. Better to have him down there than stirring him up. He's liable to go back to the parlor."

"He a smart ole…."

"Dammit, Emma! Please don't tell me that again."

"Yassum."

"How 'bout bringing me our phone book, Emma, and bring the magnifying glass."

"I thought we won't goana call nobody about the snake," Emma said.

"We're not, but I have to make another call."

When Emma returned with the phone book and magnifying glass, Miss Kate squinted as she looked through the Shaw's Pond listings. Then she dialed.

"Please put Sam Cobbett on the line," she said, staring down as she waited.

"Sam," she said moments later. "This is Kate Sims, and I need to talk to you about something very important, and I haven't laid eyes on you since the last time my boy Carter was home and you came down here to see him." Then she listened for a few seconds.

"I'd rather not talk about it over the telephone," she said and then added. "I need you to come down here, like maybe along about tomorrow. You know how close I've always been with your daddy and your granddaddy, and this is pretty important."

Seconds later: "I appreciate it Sam. Four-thirty'd be good. I'll be looking to see you at four-thirty on the dot and we'll have a cold Coca-Cola." Then she hung up and smiled. Emma looked agitated.

"Now don't forget Miss Kate, Miss Allie comin' to see us at four o'clock sharp, and Mr. Cobbett goana come at four-thirty? How you goana let that girl know her daddy'll be comin'? She talked like they ain't too close."

"I'm not gonna let her know, Emma. We'll let 'em both be surprised. It's high time they got together."

"Yassum," Emma said.

On and on, the *Bright Leaf Waltz* played. Looking out the parlor window, over the ancient boxwood and down the long dirt road, Miss Kate smiled as she began to hum along with the music and to swing her body to the rhythm. Her hand gently moved the window drape, but the jelly glass was empty.

Author's Note

My mother, Frances Hallam Hurt, herself a fine writer who died in 2015 at the age of 99, always encouraged my writing. She read only one of the stories in this collection, and her delight and laughter over the characters in "The Bright Leaf Waltz" still ring in my ears. I owe much to her as well as to my father, who introduced me to *The New York Herald-Tribune* as well as to some of the wonders of New York.

While thanking people, I happily include my past colleagues at Reader's Digest Magazine where we were all focused on the most effective way to tell a story. I think of Ed Thompson, Fulton Oursler, Marcia Rockwood, Art McManus, Steve Frimmer, Howard Dickman, Elinor Griffith, Sissi Maleki, Mary Lyn Maiscott, Nancy Tafoya and my 50-year friend, the late Ken Tomlinson. They were as good as it gets. As tough editors and researchers, they were a blessing for me as a writer.

I was particularly privileged to work with Thomas K. Noonan, the talented investigative sleuth who assisted me from time to time.

And any listing of appreciative hat tips must include my cheerful horse-loving, baby-doctoring sister, Dr. Hallam Hurt of the Children's Hospital of Philadelphia.

I also thank my friend Faye Kushner for her sharp editing assistance in readying the stories for this collection. And my appreciation to Kathleen Hurt O'Hare for her friendship in all matters literary.

As always, I am indebted to our children, Lawyer Elizabeth Hurt, Washington columnist Charlie Hurt and Congressman Robert Hurt and their families for their forthright counsel and enduring good cheer.

And, of course, my deepest thanks go to my wife Margaret who has been the steady taproot of our family at every twist and turn along the way.

Henry Hurt.
Chatham, Virginia
August, 2016